Cottage on Gooseberry Bay:

Charmed Summer

by

Kathi Daley

Gooseberry Bay

Chapter 1

"Ainsley Holloway?" a man wearing a dark brown uniform asked after he'd walked up to my cottage in Gooseberry Bay and knocked on the front door, and I'd answered.

"Yes. I'm Ainsley Holloway."

"I have a delivery for you. I've been instructed to check your ID and to have you sign for it."

"Delivery? What sort of delivery?"

The man held up an envelope. "I have this envelope and two large boxes, which I will carry up from the parking area once I've confirmed your ID and I have your signature."

I hesitated for a moment since I wasn't expecting a delivery. Being a private investigator, I tended to have a suspicious nature, which caused all sorts of weird scenarios to run through my mind up to and including a bomb in a box. I supposed I could decline to accept the delivery, but my curiosity got the better of me, so I showed the man my brand new Washington State driver's license and then signed the receipt he presented.

He handed me the envelope and then turned to retrieve the boxes. Deciding to wait where I was, I looked down at the envelope which appeared to have been sent from a law office in Northern Italy. The packages must have come from Warren Cromwell, a man I supposed might be my closest living relative. I'd spoken to him on the phone two weeks ago, and he'd mentioned that he had some photos and mementos he felt I'd like to have.

Once the delivery man returned with the boxes, I instructed him to set them inside the cottage, near the front door. I grabbed my purse, tipped the man, and then stood perfectly still as I allowed a wave of emotion to wash over me.

Seven months ago, I'd come to Gooseberry Bay looking for answers to a past which no longer made sense. My father, a career cop turned private investigator after he retired, had been shot in the line of duty and eventually died as the result of his injury. After his death, while cleaning out his attic in preparation for the sale of his house, I'd found a photo of two little girls with a blond-haired woman on the porch of a house overlooking the sea. I didn't recognize the porch or the house, but for some reason, once I'd found the photo, I'd begun to have dreams.

Vivid dreams. Dreams that, over time, I decided were real memories.

Six months ago, I'd met Adam Winchester, the eldest of the Winchester brothers. As it turned out, Adam and his brother, Archie, owned the mansion where the photo had been taken. With Adam's help, I'd been able to determine that the two little girls were, in fact, myself, who at the time had been known as Ava, and my sister, Avery. We also figured out that the woman with us was a distant relation by marriage to Adam and Archie, although neither had ever met her.

I slit the top of the envelope open to find a thick document, along with a handwritten note from Warren inside. My heart pounded, and my stomach knotted up as I read the note and considered the document. Closing my eyes, I took a deep breath and willed myself to relax by counting backward from twenty.

As I counted, I let my mind take me back to five months ago when Adam had helped me weed through the hundreds of random photos and documents stored away in the mansion he and his brother had inherited after their parents had died. I knew our quest to figure out who I'd been and what might have happened to me after the photo on the porch had been taken was a longshot. Our hope had been that we'd find clues as to why the woman, who we eventually identified as Marilee Wentworth, spent part of the summer of nineteen ninety-five at Piney Point, with two children who we determined were my sister, Avery, and me. Finding even one clue had taken us hours and hours of working together in Adam's suite at the mansion. It was time that I'd found to be both frustrating and hugely rewarding. The answers we sought had come to us slowly, and to this day, were incomplete, but during the long days and late nights we'd worked together, Adam and I had gotten to know one another and had forged a friendship.

When Adam made a trip overseas three months ago, he'd managed to track down the identity of my biological parents, a couple named Arthur and Adora Macalester. Before dying in a small plane crash in nineteen ninety-five, the couple lived on the family estate in Northern Italy with their two children, Ava (me), who was three at the time, and Avery, who was just one. The story of how the three-year-old orphan of a rich and influential European couple ended up being raised by a single cop living in Savanah, Georgia, is a long and complicated one that I'm still trying to unravel. Adam has been helping me with this endeavor, and so far, we've actually been able to figure out quite a lot.

After Arthur and Adora's deaths, Arthur's cousin, Marilee, a Massachusetts native on his mother's side, was sent to Italy to care for Ava and Avery. A man named Warren Cromwell, a local cousin on their father's side, had taken over the management of the couple's financial assets as well as the family estate on the children's behalf. For reasons I still don't understand, Marilee became convinced that not only had Warren tampered with the plane that had killed Arthur and Adora but that he had plans to do away with Ava and Avery as well. It was because of those fears that she took the children and fled to America, where they'd spent the summer of nineteen ninety-five at the home of Adam and Archie's father, Kingston. When summer came to an end, Marilee and another woman, known only as Wilma, took the children and once again fled. After leaving Piney Point, none of the four had ever heard from until I showed up looking for answers seven months ago.

My story seems to hit a wall at this point. All I know is that in December of nineteen ninety-five, I went to live with the cop who raised me, and any memories I'd had from my life before that point seemed to have been buried in my subconscious until I found the photo and a door that had been closed for a quarter of a century began to open. While my life between leaving Piney Point in August and being taken in by the man who raised me in December is still unavailable to me, with Adam's help, I have uncovered quite a bit about my life before leaving Italy for the final time.

I was jarred from my musings by a second knock on the door. I assumed the delivery man had forgotten something and reached for the door handle, but when I opened it, I found my good friend, Jemma Hawthorn, standing on the deck.

"Jemma!" I screeched, stepping forward to hug her. "You're back."

She hugged me in return. "Yes, I'm back. I actually just arrived."

I stepped aside. "Come in." I closed the door as my Bernese Mountain Dogs, Kai and Kallie, greeted one of their favorite people. "How was your trip?"

Jemma had spent the past four weeks with her father and her sister in the hope of mediating a quickly escalating conflict.

"Exhausting," Jemma answered.

"Well, have a seat and tell me all about it."

I knew that Jemma's father had met and begun dating a much younger woman who seemed to make him happy but also seemed to be bleeding him dry financially. Jemma's sister, Jackie, was concerned that this woman, who she assumed to be a gold digger, would drain their father's life savings before slithering away, never to be seen or heard from again. Jackie had been nagging Jemma to join her in an intervention for months, and Jemma, who worked remotely and could really work from anywhere, finally agreed to come home for an extended visit. She'd been gone almost a month, and I'd only spoken to her briefly during that time.

"The condensed version of a very long story is that I managed to dig up some dirt on our father's girlfriend, and my sister and I used that dirt to convince her to leave. Dad, of course, is heartbroken, but at least what's left of his savings is secure."

"So you found out that she really was after his money?" I asked.

Jemma nodded. "I was able to dig up information about past relationships. It seems that she looks for lonely widowers with a decent amount of wealth, but not too much so that they'd be naturally suspicious of newcomers in their lives. Once she chooses a target, she establishes a relationship with them. Once the relationship is cemented, she begins to challenge the man not only to step out of his comfort zone in terms of the activities he participates in, such as taking up skydiving, but she convinces him to take financial risks as well, which she then manages and controls. In the end, I suppose the man is left with the memory of a few fun months and a second chance at youth, but he's also left with a lot of empty space where his life savings used to be."

"So she moves on once the money is gone."

Jemma nodded. "Exactly."

"I'm so sorry you had to go through that."

"Me too," Jemma sighed. "At this point, Dad doesn't know that my sister and I are behind his new girlfriend leaving town so abruptly. I know she would have eventually left, and, in a roundabout way, she admitted as much. Still, I'm terrified he'll find out that we interfered. I feel like we did the only thing we could since trying to convince him that the love of his life was a gold digger was getting us nowhere, but if he finds out what we did, he'll never forgive us."

"So did the girlfriend agree that she wouldn't tell him why she was leaving?" I asked.

"I paid her a significant amount of money to tell Dad that she'd simply decided it was time to move on. I think deep down, he knew that she was the sort to do just that, so I think he believed her. At least I hope he did." She glanced at the boxes still stacked by the door. "Are you mailing something?"

"Actually, the boxes are from Warren."

Jemma looked as surprised as I'd felt when they'd been delivered. "If Warren is sending you boxes, I must have missed something."

"Actually, you've missed a lot." I pulled a bottle of wine off the rack. "Let's retire to the deck, and I'll catch you up."

"Okay. That sounds good to me. I've really missed our afternoon chats over a glass of wine."

Once we'd both been served, we toasted Jemma's return to Gooseberry Bay after a month away, and then I began my story.

"I assume you remember that before you left for your trip home, Adam had gone to Switzerland to speak to a man named Joseph Accardi."

Jemma nodded. "I do remember that. Joseph Accardi had been the Macalester family attorney at the time of Arthur and Adora's deaths. Accardi had since retired and had moved from Italy to Switzerland, which is why Adam went to Switzerland."

"Exactly. Adam was able to speak to the man and verify that Warren had gone to his cousin with a statement from the daughter of the midwife who'd delivered Leopold and Leora before Arthur's death. According to the midwife's daughter, who had been present at the birth, it had indeed been the female twin who was born first."

"I remember this as well," Jemma said. "I think you mentioned it in one of your phone calls. You and Adam were questioning the truth of Marilee's claim that Warren had killed your parents and was out to eliminate both Ava and Avery as well. You mentioned that Adam was investigating the idea that Warren had already spoken with Arthur about the birth order of Leopold and Leora before Arthur's death."

"That's all correct. Nicolas Macalester was both Arthur and Warren's grandfather, and he controlled the land and the family fortune at the time. He wanted a male heir, so he paid the midwife a lot of money to switch the times on the birth certificates, allowing Leopold rather than Leora to inherit the Macalester land and fortune on his death. This much seems to be true, but Adam wanted confirmation that Warren knew that Arthur had been made aware of the switch and had altered the trust documents before his death. This is the point where Adam had the idea to speak to Accardi, who confirmed that Arthur had been made aware of the situation and had worked out a deal with Warren that benefitted both men."

"So the story Marilee told to the family about Warren first tampering with your parent's plane and then threatening to kill you and Avery was total fiction."

"It looks likely that's the case. Accardi was able to confirm that Arthur and Warren had agreed to put the land owned by the Macalester family into a different type of family trust before Arthur's death. This trust would be managed like a corporation, with every Macalester heir owning stock in the company. Arthur and Warren were both wealthy men at this point, so they both agreed to keep their own liquid assets. It was really only the land and the vineyard that both men wanted and the land and vineyard that both men agreed to share."

"So if Warren and Arthur had worked this all out before Arthur died, then why did Marilee leave Italy with you and Avery?"

"We aren't sure at this point, although after personally speaking to Warren, I have a theory."

Jemma set her glass of wine on the table and leaned forward. "You actually spoke to this man?"

I nodded. "Once Adam and I decided that it was unlikely that Warren had reason to want Avery and me dead, he set up a video conference between the three of us. We started by explaining who I was to Warren, and I have to admit that he was both shocked and delighted to see me."

"So what did he think was going on when Marilee left with you?" Jemma asked.

"I'm getting to that."

"Sorry. Go on."

"Basically, long story short, after Marilee had been in Italy for a few months, she went to Warren and told him that she had decided to take Ava and Avery to the United States. Her family was there, and she knew she'd have help raising the girls, which at the time, Marilee admitted that she felt like she needed. Warren agreed that it might be for the best since the girls were so young, and he was unmarried at the time and had no way to look after them. Marilee asked if there was a way the money Ava and

Avery had inherited could be put in a trust with her as the administrator since she would be the one to bear the weight of the financial burden of raising them. Remember that at this point, the land was already in the process of being transferred to the family company Arthur and Warren had agreed upon, but Arthur had a lot of other money and assets that Warren was managing on behalf of his nieces. Warren shared with Adam and me that he wasn't comfortable signing the entire estate over to Marilee to manage on our behalf. He did, however, want to make sure that both Avery and I had everything we needed, so he set up accounts in each of our names into which he made monthly deposits and Marilee controlled."

Jemma held up a hand. "Wait. Warren donated money to an account on your behalf every month after Marilee left Italy with you? Is the money still there?"

I shook my head. "No. At least not that money. Hang on, and I'll get there."

"Okay. Sorry. Go on."

"Anyway, Marilee left with Avery and me, promising to stay in touch with Warren, and Warren began making monthly deposits of ten thousand dollars into each of our accounts."

"Ten thousand dollars a month!"

"I know that sounds like a crazy amount of money for a one and three-year-old, but that's what Warren told me. Keep in mind that this was money left to us by our parents. Warren was just managing it."

"Okay. Go on."

"I knew that I was with the cop who raised me by December of the same year the cash infusions began, so I asked Warren if he knew what had happened to the money. He told Adam and me that he didn't know how the funds were used and had no idea that Avery and I were missing. He also shared that he had continued to add money to the accounts until twenty eleven."

"Why did he stop in twenty eleven?" Jemma asked.

"When I turned eighteen in twenty ten, Warren asked Marilee to put me in contact with him. He wanted to change the account, so I had direct control of it. She stalled for almost a year, and when she never would comply with his request, he stopped adding funds to both accounts."

Jemma held up her palm again. "Okay, wait. Marilee seemingly dropped you off in Savannah in nineteen ninety-five, and as far as we know, no one ever saw her again, but Warren continued to communicate with her, and he continued to send her money?"

I nodded. "Marilee, or someone pretending to be Marilee, sent Warren annual updates on both Avery and me, which were totally fake. At least the updates about me were fake. I can't be sure if Marilee stayed in contact with Avery. The thing is that the communiqués were via email, so I guess that someone who knew the basics of the situation could have been pretending to be Marilee."

"So the whole time you were living in Georgia with your father, Warren thought you and Avery were with Marilee."

I nodded once again.

"Wow."

"I know. It's crazy. Warren admitted that he should have physically checked on us, but he was busy, and shortly after Marilee left with us, he married and had a family of his own. He was putting ten grand in my account and ten grand in Avery's account, and someone was taking the money out each month. He assumed it was being used to raise us in the upper-class society we were born into."

"So, at what point did Warren begin to believe that you weren't with Marilee after all?" Jemma asked.

"After he stopped adding money to the two bank accounts, he expected that I, who was nineteen by this point, and Avery, who was seventeen, would reach out to him. Warren thought it might take a while, but he figured that someone would come around looking for more once the balance in the accounts dried up. No one ever did. He looked for Marilee at this point, but her family told him that she hadn't been seen or heard from in years. He then looked for Avery and me but came up totally empty. It was at this point that he began to suspect that all of us were dead and that someone else had been draining the accounts each month."

"Is that what you think happened?" Jemma asked me.

"I don't know. I know I'm not dead, but I suppose for all intents and purposes, Ava Macalester has been dead since nineteen ninety-five. As for Marilee and Avery, I hope they are alive, but I'm no closer to figuring that out than I was when this whole thing started."

Jemma tucked her feet up under her body. "I hate to say it, but it sounds like Marilee is the bad guy in all of this."

"Yeah," I sighed. "Adam and I discussed the fact that it really does look like she made up the whole thing about Warren killing my parents and being a threat to Avery and me so that the family would help her with us while she made away with our money. If I had to guess, she pawned both Avery and me off on kind and caring people in her life who would want to protect an innocent child, and then she spent the next sixteen years draining our bank accounts every month."

"So why did she take you from Piney Point? Why give you to someone all the way in Georgia?"

"Adam and I aren't sure, but if you remember, once she took us to Piney Point, she left and only popped in now and then. It was Winnie who took care of us. Adam suspects that Marilee was away making arrangements for the money during this time. He also suspects that someone in the family might have begun to suspect something was off, which caused Marilee to take us somewhere where no one would know who we really were. Either that or Marilee had a partner who was actually calling the shots. There's still a huge void understanding what happened to us after we left Piney Point."

"So if that's true, it's quite possible that Avery really is out there living the life she was handed with no idea who she actually is."

"Probably," I said. "Avery was just one year old when this all happened. I have limited memories that seem to randomly filter through, but she won't have any. If she is alive, and I hope she is, I plan to try to find her. I have no idea how I'm going to do that, but I'm going to try."

"And Marilee?" Jemma asked.

I shrugged. "I imagine Marilee is either dead or in the wind. No one in the family has seen or heard from her for years. Wilma either."

Jemma picked up her wine and took a sip. "Talk about a crazy story."

"Yeah." I thought about the boxes. "But it hasn't been all bad. Warren is a really nice man, as is his wife, Giovanna. I hope to meet them both in person soon. Plus, Warren told me that he has been hanging onto the money Avery and I inherited. It's just sitting in a bank, waiting for one of us to claim it."

"Are you going to claim it?"

"I don't know. I guess maybe eventually. I would rather wait until Avery is found. In the meantime, Warren set up an account for me that I have access to so that I can make a withdrawal any time I need. He sent an envelope with information about this account as well as financial statements relating to the cash and investments he's been managing for Avery and me. I haven't had a chance to really look them over, but it appears that I really do have a lot of money."

"It almost sounds as if you think this is a bad thing."

I shrugged. "It feels strange to even think about using any of this money. I don't feel like Ava Macalester. I feel like Ainsley Holloway. And even if I could convince myself it really was mine, what would I do with it? I certainly don't need it."

Jemma untucked her legs. "I guess it's nice to know it's there if you ever do need it."

"Yeah. I guess. I suppose it's odd that while I'm not really all that thrilled about the money, I am thrilled to find out that I'm related to Warren and Giovanna. Since Adam first told me about them, I've spent hours stalking them on the internet. I was obsessed with learning everything that I could about them. Initially, I was looking for confirmation that the guy was the lowlife Marilee had told the family he was, but what I found was a really great guy who seems to use his money and influence to benefit his village. Not only does he give of his time and his money, but there are dozens and dozens of photos of the couple attending fundraisers and ribbon cuttings, as well as very high-end parties and exclusive events. It's almost like they're royalty."

"It sounds like they are royalty in their own little corner of the world." Jemma glanced at her watch. "I'm supposed to meet Booker at the marina at five. He wants to talk to me about a birthday gift for

Tegan, so we're going to have a drink. Do you want to come along?"

"Are you sure he won't mind?"

"He won't mind. I guess there's a specific gift he wants to get Jemma, but it's one of those items that are hard to find, so he's hoping I can use my computer magic to track one down online. He wanted me to meet him, so he wouldn't have to make an excuse for coming to the cottage to talk to me without Tegan tagging along."

I slid my legs to the side to stand up. "Okay. I'll go with you. Let me run a brush through my hair."

Once I tidied up a bit, I let the dogs out for a quick bathroom break, and then Jemma and I headed toward the marina.

"I wonder what's going on," Jemma said after we'd noticed Deputy Todd talking to a group of teenagers on the beach who appeared to have been out paddleboarding.

"I don't know. It looks like everyone is standing around that blue paddleboard, although I can't tell who it belongs to. It looks as if everyone in the group has their paddleboard."

Jemma narrowed her gaze and then nodded toward the parking area for the marina. "It looks like Parker is here."

Parker Peterson is a friend of ours who also happens to be the best reporter in town. If Parker decided to show up, then chances were that Deputy Todd was talking to the group on the beach about something more important than littering or unsafe roughhousing.

"I'm going to text Parker and let her know we're up here in the parking area. Maybe she can stop by when she's done with Todd and fill us in," Jemma informed me.

I watched as Parker headed straight toward Deputy Todd. She said something to him, and he nodded, glancing toward the blue paddleboard on the sand. She said something else, and one of the boys Todd had been talking with pointed out toward the eastern shore of the bay. Parker commented again, and Deputy Todd knelt down on the sand to take a closer look at the paddleboard. Jemma and I couldn't hear what was being said by anyone involved in the conversation, but it did appear that the blue paddleboard was the topic of conversation.

After about fifteen minutes, Parker turned away from the group and headed toward where Jemma and I were waiting.

"What's going on?" Jemma asked when Parker sat down next to us.

"Zane Maddox was reported missing by his mother this morning," she answered. "Apparently, he went out paddleboarding yesterday afternoon but never returned." Parker looked at me. "Zane is a fifteen-year-old and the youngest son of Harold Maddox."

I knew that Harold Maddox was one of the members of the town council. I seemed to remember that Harold's family had lived in Gooseberry Bay for generations.

"I take it the blue paddleboard belonged to him," I said.

"Yes," Parker confirmed. "When Zane was last seen, he was leaving home with his blue paddleboard. His parents told Deputy Todd that they were pretty sure he planned to meet up with some other kids from the high school, but Zane didn't specifically say who he was meeting."

"So, how are the teens on the beach involved?" I asked.

"They're the ones who found the paddleboard floating in the bay. There's a chip on one end of the paddleboard that looks new. Although Deputy Todd doesn't know if the paddleboard was damaged during whatever occurred to cause Zane to go missing or if it was washed up onto some rocks at some point after whatever happened to Zane occurred."

"So what does Deputy Todd think happened to Zane?" Jemma asked.

"He has no idea at this point. Given the fact that his paddleboard was found floating in the middle of the bay, it appears he may have drowned, but without a body, there's no way to know that for sure."

"I guess Deputy Todd will open a case and look into it," I said.

"Yeah," Parker agreed. "That's the plan. He mentioned trying to track down whomever Zane met up with yesterday. Someone must have seen him. If he can figure out where Zane went after he left home, that will at least give him a starting point." She glanced away from the water. "So what are the two of you up to?"

"We're supposed to meet Booker for a drink, but the walkway to the marina's office is blocked by the two cops who seem to be herding people away from Deputy Todd and the group he's talking to," Jemma said.

I glanced back toward the beach where the group that had gathered had begun to break up. Deputy Todd was carrying the paddleboard toward his car, and the teens that had gathered began wandering off in different directions.

"It looks like Todd is about to be freed up," Parker said, turning and trotting in his direction.

"Did you know Zane?" I asked Jemma.

"Not really, but I know who he is, and I've chatted with his mom, June, a few times. June works part-time for the town and she volunteers at the library. She's a nice woman, and I know she adores her children. I hope Zane's okay."

"And Zane's father?" I asked.

"He's actually a bit of an ogre. I never really liked him or his politics."

"Does Zane have siblings?"

Jemma nodded. "He's the baby of the family, but he has a sister named Cora, who I think is a freshman in college this year. I seem to remember I heard that she was headed toward the east coast this past fall." Jemma paused, furrowing her brow slightly. She glanced back toward the beach. "I don't know Zane well, but I do know someone who might know something about what's going on."

"Oh? Who's that?"

"A boy named Artie Drysdale. Artie is Jim Drysdale's son, the man who owns the curio shop a few doors down from your office. I think Jim knows Josie from a book club the two used to belong to."

"And you think Artie might know what's going on with Zane?"

"Artie and Zane run with the same group of kids, so I think he might." She looked at her watch. "I'll text him and ask him to call me when he has a minute. I don't know for certain if he knows anything, but if he was part of the crowd Zane was supposed to meet up with, at the very least, he should know if he ever showed up."

"It seems like it might be worth looking into things. If Zane's missing and still alive rather than a drowning victim, then finding him as soon as possible is important." I glanced back toward the crowd. "Should we try to make our way over to Booker?"

"Yeah. Let's give it a try. If we can't get in for some reason, I'll text Booker and suggest he just meet us at the bar."

Chapter 2

The cops near the marina's entrance weren't letting anyone in, so Jemma texted Booker to suggest that he just meet us at the bar down the street. He indicated that he would and that he should be there shortly, so Jemma and I went ahead and set off in that direction. When we arrived at the pub where we'd arranged to meet Booker, Jemma headed to the bar for a couple glasses of wine while I snagged a table near a window.

"So, how's the PI business been treating you while I was away?" Jemma asked once we'd settled in to wait.

"It's been slow, but I knew going in that getting established would take a while."

"I guess you really don't need the money."

I thought about the bank account Warren had established for me. "No," I answered. "I guess I don't need the money, but I enjoy the challenge of taking on a new case and helping people."

"Anything interesting?"

I shrugged. "Not really interesting. I was asked to help one of the vendors on the boardwalk figure out who was vandalizing his cart at night, and after my success with Lizzy's lost cat, I've had a few lost dog cases. Oh, and a woman asked me to try to figure out where she might have left her purse. I guess she had a bunch of cash inside when she misplaced it."

"She misplaced it? Where was it?"

"She'd left it in the ladies' room at a restaurant she'd visited earlier that week. Once we retraced her steps, it was pretty easy to find. I don't know why she even needed my help, but she did seem confused, and I think having someone to talk things through with helped her remember. I didn't charge her for such a simple case, but she did give me an unopened roll of mints as a tip."

Jemma smiled. "Well, I guess everyone has to start somewhere. It sounds like your name is getting out there."

"Yeah. I feel like that first big case is just around the corner." I waved at Booker, who'd just walked in. He motioned that he was going to grab a beer, and then he crossed the room and joined us.

"Thanks for meeting with me," he said after he slipped onto the stool.

"No problem," Jemma said. "We were happy to. I think it's sweet you're going to so much trouble for Tegan's birthday."

"What are you trying to find?" I asked.

"A first edition of *The Prairie Wife Cookbook*. It was originally published in eighteen eighty-two. It wasn't super popular like Betty Crocker cookbooks, so there aren't a lot of copies out there. Tegan told me a while back that her grandmother had one, and she'd always wished she'd kept it since it reminded her of the woman who'd first taught her to cook." He pulled his phone out and showed Jemma the cover. "I tried all the ordinary places but haven't had any luck. I thought you might have more luck."

"I'm happy to take a look. Can you text me that cover?"

He nodded and did so. I wasn't sure why a meeting was required for this simple request, but I supposed Booker really did want to make sure the gift was a surprise.

"I'd also like to throw Tegan a party this year," he continued. "I hoped we could have it at your place."

"Josie and I would be happy to host. Have you settled on a theme? A guest list? A date?"

"No. I sort of hoped that you girls would just do whatever needs to be done."

I smiled. Now I knew why Booker had wanted to talk to Jemma in person.

"We'd be happy to throw Tegan a party," Jemma said. "Tegan's birthday is June third, so maybe we can have the party on Saturday the fifth. How about I check with Josie, and we come up with a plan. I'll email you the information, so you can take a look before we put anything in play."

Booker looked relieved. "Thanks. I'd appreciate that. I know Tegan will enjoy a party, but the whole thing seems sort of overwhelming."

"No problem," Jemma said.

He took a long sip of his beer.

"So, do you know anything about the missing teen?" I asked. I supposed that just because Booker worked at the marina didn't mean he knew anything, but I figured it couldn't hurt to ask.

"Not really," Booker said. "One of the guys said that he might not be the only kid missing, but he didn't elaborate, so I'm not sure who he was talking about if, in fact, it's true and there's a second victim."

"So maybe Zane was with someone when he went missing," Jemma stated.

Booker shrugged. "I'm not sure. Maybe. I'm not even sure that particular rumor is true." He looked at his watch. "I need to get going. I'm supposed to meet up with Tegan." He hugged Jemma and me. "Thanks again. I really do appreciate the help."

After Booker left, Jemma and I decided to order an appetizer to go with our wine. While we were waiting for the appetizer to be delivered, Jemma got a text from Artie.

"Artie says that he hasn't seen Zane since Friday at school. He said they sometimes hang out on the weekends, but Zane told him he was busy. Artie had no idea what he'd been busy doing, and he had no idea why Zane wouldn't have called and invited him to go paddleboarding with him if that's what he had planned since they generally went together."

"So Zane's behavior was atypical leading up to his disappearance. I wonder what he was doing."

"I don't know, but the odds are that whatever he was doing this weekend that would cause him not to hang out with his regular crowd most likely is what's behind the abandoned paddleboard."

Jemma and I decided to return home after we'd eaten our appetizer. Jemma was tired after her trip, and I wanted to look in the boxes Warren had sent, so after we arrived on the peninsula, we each went our separate way. I had so many conflicting emotions surging through my mind as I looked more closely at the financial paperwork that Warren had sent. It seemed odd to me that not only was I Ainsley Holloway, but that I was Ava Macalester as well. I really wasn't sure what to do with that. In a way, having two identities made me feel fractured.

The boxes contained photo albums, framed photos, letters, and diaries. There were also a few pieces of jewelry, a family bible, and other odds and ends Warren had saved when he'd cleaned out my parent's home. The note Warren sent explained that he had a warehouse full of furniture and other items he'd been saving for Avery and me if we ever made an appearance and that I was welcome to come and take a look at any point.

He also restated that he really felt bad about dropping the ball and not following up to make sure that Avery and I were okay. He said that Marilee seemed like a decent person, and he had no reason to believe she was anyone other than who she presented herself to be. I guessed I understood that. Warren was a busy man with his own life and his own family. When his cousin had died prematurely, he'd done as was expected of him and took over the financial reins of his estate. Marilee had seemed willing to raise the girls, and as far as Warren knew, that was exactly what she was doing.

Warren had expressed a similar sentiment when we'd spoken during our video chat. Part of me wanted to blame him for not making sure Avery and I were okay, and part of me understood why he would have assumed we were. Warren also told me that he planned to initiate his own search for Avery. Maybe with all his money and resources, he could actually find her. I planned to continue looking, but the more people who were committed to a problem, the more likely the problem would be solved.

Taking a necklace from one of the boxes, I ran a finger over the modest diamond. It was a delicate piece with a small stone and didn't look like the sort of thing my father, who'd had a lot of money his entire life, would give to the woman he loved, but perhaps the necklace had been given to Adora before she met and married my father. The boxes of keepsakes Warren had sent contained several pieces of jewelry with larger stones that I'm sure were of greater financial value, but this tiny diamond on the delicate chain seemed to speak to me. Slipping it around my neck, I worked the clasp. Once it had settled on my chest, I fingered it, trying to conjure up a memory of the woman who'd given birth to me. I was sure there were memories stored somewhere in my mind from before her death, but no matter how hard I tried, I couldn't seem to access them. Maybe I was trying too hard. Perhaps I just needed to let my memories come to me when they were ready to be felt and experienced. Maybe, if I just sat with my thoughts, the quiet of a spring night would take me where I wanted to go.

Chapter 3

I headed into my office the following day. Part of me wanted to lie around the cottage and torture myself with thoughts of the sister I so wanted to find, but another part of me knew it was best to stay busy. There didn't seem to be a lot I could do at this point. I didn't have any new leads to follow up on, and after having been home for several months, Adam was away on business. I knew this was going to be an extended trip, so I didn't expect him to return for another week or two at the very earliest. I figured that when he got home, we'd jump back into the investigation. In the meantime, I supposed that spending some time and having a presence in my new office was a good idea.

I'd decided to bring Kai and Kallie with me today, so I settled them onto the dog beds I kept on-site for their use, and then I sat down at my desk to go over the notes I'd jotted down regarding the upcoming holiday weekend and my commitment to Hope to help out with the planned activities. Hope seemed to chair most of the events the town sponsored, but I knew that she couldn't do what she did without a massive number of volunteers to help out.

"Are you Ainsley Holloway?" A young woman with curly dark hair who looked to be about my age came into the office through the front door. Kai and Kallie looked up, but they'd been trained not to approach until invited, so they stayed put for the time being.

"I am," I answered, standing up behind my desk. "How can I help you?"

"I was next door at the antique shop, and they suggested that you might be able to help me with my project."

I motioned toward the chair across from my desk. "Have a seat."

She did as I suggested.

"So, what's your name?"

"Ellery. Ellery Adams."

"Nice to meet you, Ellery. Now, what sort of project do you have?"

She held out her hand, palm side up, and presented a charm bracelet.

"A charm bracelet. It's lovely. May I?" I asked before taking it from her hand.

"I hoped you could help me track down the owner of this bracelet."

I looked up at the woman, who seemed hesitant and obviously uncomfortable with the situation. "Why don't you start at the beginning and tell me how you came to have this and why you want to find the owner. Once we get that out of the way, I should be able to tell you whether or not I can help you."

"Okay." She swallowed hard. I could see that she was nervous, and to be honest, I wasn't sure why. Tracking down the owner of a lost bracelet didn't seem the sort of thing that would cause a person a lot of anxiety. "I was adopted when I was an infant," she began in a soft voice. "My adoptive parents were wonderful people who I loved with all my heart, but they were killed in an auto accident last summer."

"I'm so very sorry." I knew how hard it was to lose a parent.

She offered me a look of thanks and then continued. "After I got over the shock of losing them, I decided to look for my biological parents. I'd asked my adoptive parents about them when I was a teenager, and all they could tell me was that I'd been abandoned in a church when I was less than a day old. The blanket my naked body was wrapped in and this charm bracelet that was found wrapped inside the blanket are the only clues they had as to my identity. I know it's not a lot to go on, but it is something. A starting point, if you will."

I looked down at the bracelet I still held. "It's a lovely bracelet." I looked at the charms, which featured a book, a ship, an ice cream cone, a tennis shoe, a movie reel, a rose, and a Ferris wheel. "Do you have reason to believe that the bracelet is in some way linked to Gooseberry Bay? The charms are pretty common."

"I'm actually not certain that the charms are linked to Gooseberry Bay, but I did notice that the tennis shoe charm has an inscription."

I looked at it more closely. "B2B with the number ninety-six under it." I looked toward the woman. "Is that significant?"

She shrugged. "I'm not sure, but I'm a runner, and my adoptive mom was a runner, and I know there is a run in Gooseberry Bay every summer called the Bay to Boardwalk Run. I suppose there are other runs that might work with B2B."

"Bay to Breakers," I said, mentioning a famous run that takes place each year in San Francisco."

"Yeah," Ellery sighed. "I did think of that. And there are others that would fit as well. A lot of them, in fact. I know it's a longshot, but I noticed the book was also inscribed."

I looked at the back of the book. "Brewster's."

"There was a bookstore named Brewster's Books here in Gooseberry Bay back in the nineteen nineties. I was born in nineteen ninety-seven, so Brewster's Books would have been around during that same time frame."

I looked down at the bracelet again. "So why do you think this bracelet was left with you, and how do you think it can help you find your biological parents?"

She hesitated.

"It's okay. Whatever you're thinking is fine. I just need to get a better feel for things."

She lowered her head and then raised it again. "I've been to Gooseberry Bay before. Five years ago with my adoptive mom. I know this is going to sound crazy, but when I arrived in this town, I felt this connection. I can't explain it, but it was just so strong. I asked my mom if I'd been here before, and she said no. I commented that it seemed familiar, and she just answered back that a lot of these little beach towns all look the same. I suppose that's true in a way, but even after we went home, I could feel the pull of this place. It was really odd. But then I went off to college, and life settled into a normal routine, and Gooseberry Bay became nothing more than a memory."

"Then your adoptive parents died, and you decided to look for your biological parents."

She nodded.

"I'm not sure why I'm so focused on Gooseberry Bay, but for some reason, when I began trying to identify the charms, Gooseberry Bay was on my mind, and it occurred to me that the tennis shoe could represent some sort of fun run or marathon. When I found out about the Bay to Boardwalk Run, I felt like I was one step closer to solving my mystery." She took a breath and continued. "Then I managed to match the book to Brewster's Books, but that was as far as I got. I came to the area to see if anyone could tell me anything else about the charms that might help me in my quest. I went to Then and Again because those who deal in antiques seem to know a lot about items from the past. The women who own the shop couldn't really help me, so they sent me to you."

I looked at the bracelet again and then handed it back to the woman. "I'm afraid that I'm new to Gooseberry Bay, so these charms won't mean anything to me, but I have friends who've been in the area longer, so I'm willing to pitch in and help you figure out as much as you can. I have to be honest, I'm not sure that even if we identify every single charm on the bracelet, doing so will help you find your biological parents. Although I do agree that it does seem like a good place to start."

"I would like to have help with my project, but I can't afford a lot, and the women next door didn't say what you charge."

I smiled. "Actually, I'm not planning to charge you anything. Your project seems important, and I, too, am looking for answers to my own past, so I understand your drive to solve this huge question in your life. I have time, so I'm happy to help see what we can figure out."

"Are you sure? I don't know how much time this might take."

"I'm sure. As I said, I'm not busy right now, and your project seems interesting."

She blew out a breath. "Thank you. I really appreciate this."

I drummed my fingers on the desk as I thought over the situation a bit. "I need to show the charms to some people I know. I don't want to take the bracelet, but I would like to take close-up photos of each charm."

"Okay."

"After we do that, I'll take down your contact information. I'll check in with you each day, and we can assess the situation. Are you staying in the area?"

"I'll be here through the weekend. I live in Seattle and need to be back to work next Monday, so I plan to take the ferry back Sunday."

"Okay, then. Let's see what we can figure out between now and Sunday." I held out my hand for the bracelet so I could take the photos. "Is there anything else you can tell me that might help us?"

"Like what?" she asked.

"You said you were found in a church. Which church?"

"It was a small community church about an hour north of Seattle. It's no longer there. I checked."

"So you were abandoned near Seattle, but you think your biological parents lived here?"

"Either lived here or visited here. I'm not sure. I realize that I don't have much of a starting place, and my quest is most likely going to end in disappointment, but I need to try."

"I get it," I said. And I did. I'd started my quest to learn about my biological parents with nothing more than a photo, and look how far I'd gotten. Maybe we could pull off the same miracle for Ellery. "Tell me about the blanket you were found wrapped up in."

"It's white with these little red roses stitched along the hem. The stitch work is really intricate. It looks to be hand-stitched to me."

"Do you have the blanket with you?"

She nodded. "It's back in my hotel room. I can bring it the next time we meet."

"Okay. I don't know if the blanket holds a clue, but we don't have a lot to go on, so every little detail helps. Is there anything else you know?"

She slowly shook her head. "I don't think so."

I finished photographing the charms and handed the bracelet back to her. "Okay. Give me a day to look into things, and then I'll call you, and we can reevaluate. If all the charms relate to a place or event as we suspect the shoe and the book do, then it shouldn't be all that hard to track down the rest."

"That's what I'm hoping." She stood up with the bracelet clutched in her hand. "And thank you. I might have eventually been able to figure all this out on my own, but I welcome the help. I figure even if I don't find the woman who'd given birth to me, taking this journey might still help me to know her."

"I agree that if nothing else, tracing the charms back to the relevant event they represent should help you know the woman who owned the bracelet."

After Ellery left, I decided to take a break and take the dogs for a walk down the boardwalk. It was a gorgeous sunny day with only the hint of a breeze to ripple the water. I had to admit that Ellery's quest was an interesting one. I could understand her logic, but I really wasn't sure that finding someone who clearly didn't want to be found was going to be possible even with the clues we had. Of course, I had even fewer clues in my search for Avery, but I knew that even without a single clue to work from, I was never going to give up. I felt like I understood Ellery. We were after similar things. I almost felt as if fate had sent Ellery to me and that maybe her search for her past would somehow end up bringing me closer in my search for mine.

Chapter 4

After I got home, I headed to Jemma and Josie's place with my phone in hand. I figured they might be able to help me identify some of the charms, so I'd called earlier, and Jemma had told me to come on over with the photos. When I arrived, both roommates were on their large deck overlooking the water with a bottle of wine and tray full of snacks.

"I guess you heard that Zane Maddox isn't the only missing teenager," Josie commented as soon as I sat down.

"No. I hadn't heard. I was down by the harbor yesterday with Jemma when Deputy Todd was there talking to the group who found Zane's paddleboard, but I haven't heard anything since."

Josie tucked her tan legs up under her body. "It turns out that another boy, Kalen West, was last seen by his mother on Saturday, although she waited to contact the police until after she'd heard about Zane."

"Why'd she wait?" I asked.

Josie shrugged. "I heard that there'd been friction in the family since Kalen's parents decided to divorce, so she may have thought Kalen simply took off. I don't know this to be true with any degree of certainty, but one of my waitresses at the Rambling Rose mentioned that Kalen might not actually be missing but may have simply needed a break from things at home."

"Do you know if Kalen and Zane were together Sunday?" I asked.

"No one I've spoken to knows one way or another," Josie provided. "I suppose Parker might know more about the whole thing than we do. Maybe I'll call and invite her to come over."

"If you want to be sure she shows, tell her that we're making margaritas," Jemma suggested.

As it turned out, Parker had found out additional information about the missing boys and was happy to come by and share what she knew in exchange for an ice-cold margarita. She indicated that she needed to finish up a few things and would be by in an hour. Josie decided we should have food to go with our margaritas, so she went inside to figure out what she could make with the ingredients she had on hand.

"I hate to say it, but two missing boys feels like foul play," I said to Jemma. "One missing teen who seemed to have been separated from his paddleboard could very well indicate an accident of some sort, but if the two boys were together, it seems unlikely they both fell off."

"I suppose they could have been knocked off," Jemma suggested. "Maybe they encountered a shark or even a whale. Shark attacks don't happen very often in the bay, but we have had pods of Orcas stop by from time to time."

"Do you think that's what happened?" I asked.

She slowly lifted a shoulder. "I really don't know. It was just a guess as to how two teens could have been killed on the water without foul play being involved."

By the time Parker arrived, Josie had a pot of spicy chili verde ready to serve, with warm tortillas, cheese, and sour cream. She also had tortilla chips and salsa to go with the margaritas. I really admired the way Josie could just whip something together even if she hadn't planned to have company. She really was an amazing chef, and she seemed to have a knack for the perfect combinations.

"Something smells wonderful, and I'm starving," Parker said the minute she walked in through the front door.

"It's ready, so let's serve ourselves, and we can talk while we eat."

"That sounds good to me." Parker grabbed a bowl and served herself a generous helping.

"So you said there's another missing boy," Jemma said once we'd all served ourselves and had taken seats at the table.

"Two, actually." Parker took a sip of her margarita and then continued. "When Kalen West left home Saturday morning, he told his mother that he was meeting up with some friends and would most likely just crash with one of them since it was the weekend. Kalen and his mother haven't been getting along since his parents decided to divorce. Kalen was close to his father, and he blames his mother for him leaving even though most of the people I've spoken to who are close to the situation all agree that the breakup of the marriage was the result of multiple counts of Kalen's father's infidelity."

"So Kalen's mother didn't have reason to worry when he didn't come home Saturday evening," I surmised.

"She did not. She's currently working two jobs to make ends meet, and from what I understand, she's pretty much at the end of her rope physically and emotionally. Kalen's anger with her and the punishment he's been doling out has caused a bad situation to be even worse. When she spoke to Deputy Todd, she said she was actually relieved he was going to be away for the weekend."

"Didn't she start to worry when he didn't come home Sunday evening?" I asked.

Parker shook her head. "She told Todd that Kalen sometimes crashes with a friend Sunday nights, but until this week, he's always managed to get himself to school Monday."

"Did she know he was absent today?" Jemma asked.

"Not until she heard about Zane and called the school to check on him. When she found out that he hadn't made it to school today, she called Deputy Todd."

"Okay," I said. "So Kalen was last seen Saturday morning, and Zane was last seen last Sunday afternoon when he told his mother he was heading out to go paddleboarding."

"That's correct. When I spoke to Todd earlier, he didn't think the two cases were related despite the fact that both missing boys are fifteen-year-olds who attend the local high school, but then shortly before I left the office to come over here, I found out that a third boy, Trevor Wilson, never made it home from school today."

"So does it look as if he was abducted?" Josie asked.

"Todd didn't know. Trevor was last seen leaving school on his bike at three o'clock. He was grounded after getting in trouble for breaking curfew over the weekend and told to come straight home after school let out. When he didn't show up at home, his father went looking for him, but so far, he's been unable to find him."

"So now we have three missing kids," Jemma said. "All boys, all fifteen, all students at Gooseberry High. This can't be a coincidence."

"At this point, Deputy Todd is beginning to suspect that all three boys have been abducted," Parker confirmed.

"Were they friends?" I asked.

"Not really," Parker replied. "Zane is an athlete and tended to hang out with the jocks, Kalen played sports in the past but wasn't nearly as committed as Zane, and it appears he dropped off the teams he'd participated with last year. Based on what I've been able to find out, once Kalen's father left, Kalen began hanging out with the gang at the auto shop. And Trevor is a genius of sorts who hung out with an academic crowd."

"So, is there any way we can help?" I asked.

Parker hesitated. "You know how I like to be in the middle of things, but Todd is talking about bringing in the FBI. We are, after all, talking about three missing kids. If the FBI does get involved, I seriously doubt that they would tolerate any outside interference the way Todd can usually be convinced to."

"So you aren't going to investigate?" Josie asked Parker.

"I didn't say that. But if we are going to poke around, we'll need to be discrete. And careful. Even more careful than usual."

Josie, Jemma, and I all agreed we were there for Parker if she needed us.

After Parker finished her meal and left, Jemma asked me about the charms I'd come by to show them in the first place. I shared the story of my new client and her quest to find her biological parents. There wasn't a lot to go on at this point, but she did have the charm bracelet and the blanket, which I described in detail.

"I took photos of the charms on the bracelet. Do any of them mean anything to you? Keep in mind that the date on the shoe is ninety-six, so it might be possible that all the charms were collected around that time."

"Some charm bracelets take years to complete," Josie pointed out.

"That's true, but Ellery was born in nineteen ninety-seven, and the shoe has ninety-six stamped beneath B2B, so at this point, we're assuming the person who owned the bracelet was involved in the Bay to Boardwalk Run in nineteen ninety-six. Of course, we don't know that with any degree of certainty. There are other runs that would work with B2B, and I suppose it's even possible that the ninety-six means something else entirely."

"How exactly does your client think that this charm bracelet is going to help her find her biological parents?" Jemma asked. "Does she have a theory?"

"I'm not sure. My client told me that she was left in a small community church just hours after her birth in April of nineteen ninety-seven. She was wrapped in a white blanket with red roses stitched along the hem but was otherwise naked. The charm bracelet was tucked into the blanket, so I guess she figures that if her biological mother went to all the trouble to leave the charm bracelet behind, it must be significant. I think my client realizes that finding her biological mother based on clues provided in a charm bracelet is a longshot, but I also think she realizes that other than the blanket, the bracelet is the only clue she has."

"Maybe your client's biological mother had a summer romance in nineteen ninety-six which led to her becoming pregnant with your client. What's her name?" Josie asked.

"Ellery."

"Maybe Ellery hopes that she can use the charms as clues to recreate her mother's movements that summer," Josie continued. "Maybe she hopes that someone will recognize the bracelet and remember her mother."

"I guess it's possible," Jemma admitted. She looked at me. "You know, if Ellery's mother participated in the Bay to Boardwalk Run in nineteen ninety-six, we might be able to get a list of participants for that year. I'm assuming one existed at the time, and if it was digitized, which I would assume by that point it would have been, it may still exist."

"It could provide a starting point," I agreed. "Assuming, of course, that the shoe represents that specific run and that the bracelet did, in fact, belong to Ellery's mother. Can you access the list?"

Jemma shrugged. "I can try." She got up, crossed the room, and picked up her laptop. She returned to the sofa, tucking her legs up under her body and settling the laptop on her lap. She then began to type. I knew this might take a while, so I turned my attention to Josie.

"The other charm that we feel fairly certain about is the book," I said to Josie. "The book has the name Brewster's inscribed on it. Ellery did some research and discovered that there had indeed been a bookstore named Brewster's Books in Gooseberry Bay back in the nineties."

"Sure. I remember that place. It was located in the building where the museum is now housed."

"How long ago did it go out of business?" I asked.

Josie paused and then answered. "Maybe four or five years ago, I guess. The little store lasted longer than some of the other independents in the area, but the owner, a woman named Kendra Hart, decided to retire, so she liquidated the stock and sold the building to the historical society."

"Does Kendra still live in the area?" I asked.

"Yes, she does. In fact, Kendra volunteers at the museum." Josie's eyes widened. "You're hoping that she'll remember the woman with the bracelet."

"It's worth asking."

"I'm off tomorrow. I'll go to the museum with you if you want. If Kendra isn't working tomorrow, whoever is should know when she'll be in. It might be a good idea to bring the actual charm bracelet when you speak to her."

"Let's confirm she's available to speak with. If she is and she wants to see the actual bracelet, I'll call my client and have her meet us there."

"Okay, guys. I have the list of entrants for the Bay to Boardwalk Run in nineteen ninety-six," Jemma said.

"That's wonderful," I said. "How long is it?"

"There were six hundred and forty-two entrants."

"Yikes!" I narrowed my gaze. "That's a lot. Can we narrow it down?"

"I eliminated the men and pulled up a list of women only, which brought it down to three hundred and eighty-four." Jemma sat staring at her screen.

"I know this is a guess, but if Ellery is correct and her mother spent the summer in Gooseberry Bay, only to end up pregnant and alone, chances are she was young. How young, I don't know, but abandoning a naked baby in a church doesn't sound like something someone with maturity would do."

"I guess I can set some age parameters. The run is open to everyone sixteen and above, so how about sixteen to twenty-two?" Jemma asked.

"That sounds like a good place to start."

She typed in the parameters we'd discussed and then sat back. "It didn't help much. There are still two hundred and four entrants."

"Okay, let's print out a list with those names," I suggested. "Let's also print the list of all the female entrants. Maybe someone will be able to remember some of these individuals. I have to assume that quite a few of them were local. We can ask around and begin to eliminate those individuals who are known to others and who definitely weren't pregnant during the winter between the summer of ninety-six and the spring of ninety-seven."

Josie sat on the sofa, thumbing through the photos on my phone. "A couple of these charms, like the shoe, if it turns out that it is associated with the Bay to Boardwalk Run, seem like they might provide a clue, but other charms, like the ice cream cone, are too common to be of much use. Even if you settled on the idea that the cone represented an ice cream shop and the shop was important to the story, which shop?"

"I suppose we can go down to the Chamber of Commerce and get a list of all the ice cream shops in Gooseberry Bay that held licenses and did business in nineteen ninety-six," I said. "There couldn't have been that many. Sure, Gooseberry Bay is a beach town which probably does have a higher ice cream shop to population ratio than some towns, but still, we're probably only looking at a handful of vendors."

"What about all the ice cream carts on the boardwalk?" Josie asked. "There are a bunch of them in the summer, and I'm not sure they have business licenses."

"I guess that's true," I admitted.

"And we don't know for certain that the ice cream cone represents an actual place. Maybe the woman who owed the bracelet simply liked ice cream."

I wrinkled my nose as I considered this idea. "There are seven charms on the bracelet. Seven memories were chosen to commemorate a summer filled with hundreds of experiences. If we're correct, and that's what was going on, I think we should assume the charms are important and not a whim."

"Like the rose," Josie said. "You said the blanket Ellery was wrapped in had roses on it, and the bracelet also has a rose. I would think that a rose is an important clue."

"Maybe, but it's also pretty general. Maybe the woman who owned the bracelet just liked roses. And even if it is an important clue and we can track it back to a flower shop, we don't know for sure that all the charms were all gathered over one summer, let alone all in Gooseberry Bay," Jemma pointed out. "Perhaps we can determine that this piece of information will help us with the remaining charms, but at this point, the only charm associated with nineteen ninety-six is the shoe."

Jemma was right. I supposed I was getting ahead of myself.

Josie continued to thumb through the photos, pausing to consider each one. "I wonder if the movie reel is supposed to commemorate Gooseberry Bay's annual Movies on the Beach event the town holds every other Friday during the summer."

"There's a movie on the beach event?" I asked.

She nodded. "A movie is shown on a huge screen made out of an old sail down on Land's End Beach every other Friday from the last Friday in June through the last Friday in August. It's a free event, and the movies are definitely not new releases, but it's fun. It's also sort of romantic since the movie doesn't start until it's completely dark."

"So it's one of those things where everyone brings their own chair or blanket," I confirmed.

"Exactly." Josie grinned. "A lot of the younger couples who show up for the food and socializing portion end up sneaking off down the beach for a bit of romance after the movie starts. I wouldn't be surprised in the least to find out that Ellery was conceived at one of the movie nights."

"It sounds fun," I said. "Kind of like a drive-in theater without the cars. And I can imagine that sitting out under the stars with your guy or gal of the moment would be very romantic. The only problem is that a movie under the stars with a make-out session on the side doesn't give us much information to go on. Not like the run that led to a list or the book we hope will lead to a woman who might remember the woman who wore the bracelet."

Josie shrugged. "I guess that's true, but maybe there's more to it." She looked at Jemma. "Can you pull up a list of movies shown on the beach during the summer of nineteen ninety-six?"

"I can try."

"Do you think the clue might be the movie?" I asked.

"It could be. If a movie called *High School Romance* or *One Long Summer* was playing, that might actually help confirm the theory you've been working from," Josie said. "That's if the title is the clue, of course. At this point, this whole thing is pretty random. I mean, it is possible that the person who left Ellery in the church, presumably her mother, just wanted her to have a memento from her, and the charms really don't mean anything."

"Yeah," I agreed. "I suppose it is equally likely that the charms aren't clues as it is that they are. But my client wants to follow that idea, and I plan to help her however it works out."

Jemma typed a series of commands into her computer. "There were five movie nights that summer," she said. "The movies featured were: *Back to the Future*, *The Karate Kid*, *The Princess Bride*, *Goonies*, and *War Games*."

"If the movie is a clue, it has to be *The Princess Bride*," Josie said.

"Probably. But I guess that isn't enough of a clue to really be a clue," I pointed out.

"What are the other charms?" Jemma asked. "In addition to the movie reel, the shoe, the rose, the book, and the ice cream cone."

"There's a ship, a large one. Maybe a cruise ship or I suppose it could even represent the ferry. There is also a Ferris wheel. I suppose that might be a reminder of a carnival if one happened to have been in town at the time."

"There is a traveling carnival that sets up down near the marina for a week in July every year," Josie said. "And they do have a Ferris wheel."

"I'm not sure knowing about the carnival will help us figure any of this out," Jemma said.

"Maybe not, but let's start with what we have," Josie suggested. "Let's talk to Kendra from Brewster's Books and see if she knows anything about the book charm. Maybe she'll remember the woman who wore the bracelet, and we'll have our baby mama without even having to figure out the other charms."

The three of us agreed to meet up tomorrow and head into town. Josie, who'd lived in the area longer than Jemma or me, knew Kendra and agreed to introduce us and ask for her help, while Jemma promised to brainstorm and try to figure out what the charms on the bracelet might relate to. I planned to work on it myself, although I really hadn't been around long enough to be able to notice associations, even if they did exist.

Chapter 5

I got up early the following morning to take the dogs for a long run. The museum opened at eleven, so I planned to meet Josie and Jemma at their cottage at ten-thirty. Most of the time, I took Kai and Kallie to the office with me, but since I would be out and about today, I decided to leave them home, hence the extra-long run. I felt my muscles warm as I settled into a steady pace. The view along the bay trail was exceptional this morning. Small fishing vessels that would stay in the bay dotted the water, but it was the large open water vessels heading out toward the channel that would take them to the sea that most enchanted me.

I loved these early mornings with the dogs. Running relaxed me. It was an activity that allowed me to challenge my body while resting my mind, which I found more and more a necessity as the answers I'd been seeking began to unfold. Sometimes, I found it difficult to quiet my thoughts, but more often than not, I found the quiet and solace I sought by being out here on the trail as the sun greeted the day.

There were actually a lot of running trails in the area, each with its own special appeal, but I found that the dogs and I most often chose the trail that hugged the bay on the south end and then climbed up onto Piney Point and the trail that led to the back fence of the estate owned by Adam and Archie. Both Winchester brothers had been out of town lately. Adam frequently traveled as part of his job as the administrator for the family foundation, but Archie tended to travel more for pleasure. The last I heard, he was heading to French Polynesia with a woman he'd met at a fundraiser he'd attended just after Valentine's Day while Adam was in Europe taking care of family business.

When the dogs and I reached the estate's back fence, I paused briefly before heading back. We'd run hard up the hill, so my plan was to mostly walk on the return trip to prevent the dogs from becoming overworked.

As I slowly began to make my way along the point toward the trail that would take me to the cottage, an image of my best friend, Keni, flashed into my mind. I'd been meaning to call her. I made a mental note to do so today. Keni had been saying that she would come for a visit for months, but so far, every time she'd set a date, she'd ended up canceling.

I missed her a lot and hoped she'd finally be able to make the commitment, but I also understood that she lived a busy life and her career as an actress came first. I was proud of Keni. She knew what she wanted, and she worked hard to get it. There was no doubt in my mind that one day her name would be plastered on billboards for the world to see and know.

As the trail flattened and began to hug the waterline, I slowed even more so the dogs could splash around. I pulled my phone out of my pocket to check the time and noticed I had a missed call from Adam. Deciding to call him back in the hope of catching him, I hit the call back button and waited.

"Adam, I'm sorry I missed your call. The dogs and I were out running, and I guess I didn't hear the phone ring."

"I should have known you might be out running. I guess it's early morning there in Gooseberry Bay."

"Where are you?" I wondered.

"Actually, I'm in New York."

"New York? I thought you were in France."

"I was, but I finished up there, so I'm heading back home via the east coast. I have a shareholders meeting Thursday for a company I hold a significant amount of stock in, and then I have a gala to attend in Boston Saturday. I was going to head home after that, but I had dinner with the president of a private children's hospital I partially fund last night, and she managed to persuade me to stay around long enough to attend a fundraiser they have planned for the following weekend."

"So you'll be home after that?"

"I will. I haven't made plane reservations yet, but you should expect me in about two weeks."

"I look forward to it."

"So, how are things going? Any new developments with your origin story?"

When the dogs grew tired of swimming, we started to slowly walk back toward the cottage while I talked.

"Not really. Although I did receive two boxes of mementos, along with an envelope full of financial information, and a note from Warren yesterday."

"It was nice of him to send all that along."

"It was," I agreed. "I have to admit I'm feeling a bit overwhelmed. In fact, overwhelmed is too tame a word for what I'm feeling."

"It's okay to take things slowly," he reminded me. "Go through the boxes when you feel ready. The items contained within will keep. As for the financial stuff, Warren has been managing things all this time, and I suspect he's willing to continue to do so for as long as you want him to. Let him do so. You need time to ease yourself into your new situation."

I paused and looked out at the bay. "I intend to let Warren manage the money and stocks and whatever else I own. I don't feel ready to take on such a thing, and, to be honest, I'm not even sure I want the responsibility for all that. What am I going to do with so much money?"

"I guess you can eventually donate it. Maybe you can even establish a charitable foundation or, perhaps you can piggyback on the one Warren and Giovanna already established. But for now, like I said, I'd just let it be. I remember how overwhelmed I was when my parents died, and I became responsible for managing the assets. It was terrifying, and I'd grown up knowing that one day the Winchester fortune would be mine and Archie's to deal with, so I do understand how you're feeling. Warren seems like a good man who knows what he's doing. If he's willing to continue to handle things, that gives you time to really think about things and decide what to do."

I started walking again. "Yeah. I guess that's true. And to be honest, I'd really like to find Avery before I make any huge decisions. Half of those assets do belong to her. If she's still alive, I'd like her to be able to help me decide what to do next."

"We'll keep looking for Avery," Adam assured me.

"I know. And maybe we'll actually find her. There are times when I want to give up due to the impossible nature of the quest, but I started with only a photo and have gotten as far as I have in less than a year, so maybe miracles do happen."

"I know they do. Listen, I need to go. My driver is here. I'll call you in a couple days, and you feel free to call me any time you need to talk."

"Okay. I just might do that if it starts to feel like the walls are closing in. Enjoy the rest of your trip."

"I will. Enjoy your sunny day in Gooseberry Bay."

"How do you know it's sunny here?"

"My weather app on my phone."

I smiled. "Yeah, I guess that will keep you up to date on the latest weather changes. I'll see you in two weeks." With that, I hung up.

Once the dogs and I arrived back at the cottage, I gave them food and water, and then I headed to the shower. Since I had an hour or so before I had to meet up with Jemma and Josie, I had time to have a cup of coffee and scramble an egg. Once I'd showered and dressed, I headed out onto the deck with my breakfast. It really was another beautiful day in paradise.

Kai and Kallie were tired from our run, so they were happy to lay in the shade while I relaxed in my lounger. I thought about the charms as I sipped my coffee. I knew that the list from the Bay to Boardwalk Run was too extensive to be of much use, but if we had a second list to compare it to, perhaps a second event our charm bracelet owner participated in, we might be able to whittle the list down significantly.

I was interested to learn what, if anything, the woman who'd owned the bookstore could tell us. If the charm had been purchased by someone who was simply a one-time customer, I doubt there was much information she'd be able to provide, but if the charm was owned by a frequent customer, maybe she'd remember her.

And then there was the movie hint. Again, even if we could figure out which movie our woman with the charm bracelet wanted to remember, I really didn't see how that could help us track her down. Unless, as I suspected, there actually was more to it. Movies on the Beach was a free event sponsored by the town, so I doubted there were employees associated with the event, but maybe volunteers. Someone had to choose the movies, run the projector, set up the screen, and clean up afterward. I might not have been living in Gooseberry Bay long, but I had been living here long enough to know that Hope Masterson was the person to ask if you had a volunteer question.

"Hope, it's Ainsley," I said after she answered my call.

"Ainsley, how are you?"

"I'm good. Really good, in fact."

"I'm so happy to hear that. How is your PI business going?"

"I feel like it's beginning to get some traction. Listen, the reason I'm calling is because I have a client who is trying to track down the owner of a charm bracelet."

"A charm bracelet? You don't say. I haven't seen one of those in ages, although they used to be quite popular."

"We have reason to believe the charm bracelet was assembled back in the nineties. Probably the mid-nineties. My client believes the charms are actually clues of a sort. One of the charms is a movie reel. I was chatting with Jemma and Josie last evening, and they told me about the annual Movies on the Beach event. They said the movies were around back then, so I'm pursuing that angle. The reason I called was to ask if the movie event is run by staff or volunteers."

"The whole thing is run by volunteers. There is a committee in charge of selecting and obtaining the movies. They set the dates and are in charge of marketing and that sort of thing. A woman named Greta Barber chairs the committee. She's a teacher at the high school during the school year, but she has quite a bit of free time during the summer, so she also takes charge of finding and supervising the volunteers who set up and run the snack bar."

"Would she have been running the event back in nineteen ninety-six?"

"She would have. In fact, she's been running this event since the late eighties when she took over for her aunt, who was also a teacher."

"I'd like to talk to her about the charm bracelet. Do you know how I can get ahold of her?"

"I guess your best bet would be to show up at the high school at three o'clock when they let out. I'm sure she'll be in her room for at least half an hour after the students leave."

"Do you know which room I'd be able to find her in?"

"She teaches drama, so just head toward the theater. There's an office in that building."

"Okay, I'll try that. Thanks."

"Before you go," Hope said. "Are you still planning to help out at the kiddie carnival in the park Saturday?"

"I have it on my calendar. You said to meet between eight and eight-thirty."

"That's still the case. Everyone is gathering at the volunteer table."

"I'll be there. Is there anything I need to bring?"

"Everything you'll need will be provided. I'll see you then, and good luck with your scavenger hunt."

In a way, I supposed that my search for the meaning behind the charms was a type of scavenger hunt, although I hadn't exactly been thinking of it that way. Realizing that I needed to get moving if I was going to meet Jemma and Josie on time, I got up and headed inside.

Chapter 6

Josie and Jemma were ready and waiting when I arrived. Josie had called ahead and spoken to Kendra Hart to confirm that she had planned to volunteer today and that she would have time to chat. The Gooseberry Bay museum was located up on a hill across from the south end of the bay. It was a brick building with a lot of charm that featured large windows and beautiful gardens. I imagined that as a bookstore, the place was charming, although it made a cozy and welcoming museum as well.

Since Josie was the one who knew Kendra the best, she introduced Jemma and me and then explained why we were there.

"I'm happy to help if I can. Do you have the charm?" Kendra asked.

"I have a photo of the charm. My client has the bracelet, but I'm sure she'd be happy to bring it by if you feel that seeing the actual bracelet is important."

She slipped her glasses on, resting them on the edge of her nose. "So let's take a look at this photo."

I pulled it up on my phone and then handed the phone to her. Perhaps I should print out the photos when I got back to my office.

"This is a reading challenge charm," she said.

"Reading challenge?" I asked.

"There was a span of maybe six or seven years where the bookstore issued a summer reading challenge. Residents and even a few summer visitors signed up, and each participant received a log to keep track of the books they read. There were spaces for the title and the author, the number of pages, a star rating, and a brief review. The bookkeeping for the challenge was strictly an honor system since we had no way to confirm such things, but in general, I think that most folks kept accurate records."

"And the participants received a charm?"

"There were prizes for various levels. If you read a thousand pages over the course of the summer, you received a bookmark signed by a local author. For reading twenty-five hundred pages, you received your choice of a mug or t-shirt, plus the bookmark. For reading five thousand pages, you received your choice of charm or key ring, plus the mug or t-shirt and the bookmark. The prizes did vary somewhat from year to year, and the prizes differed slightly each year."

"So you'd change up the design on the mug and t-shirt and maybe offer different charms," I said.

"Exactly. The charm in this photo was from the challenge in nineteen ninety-six." She pointed to the photo. "See, there's a little nine and a little six on the spine of the book represented on the charm."

I looked closely and did notice the numbers, which had been too small to really stand out amidst the design. "So, do you have records of the event?" I asked. "Would you be able to tell us who earned charms that year?"

She nodded. "I kept records of everything. They're all digitized. If you want to leave me an email address, I can send you a list of names of those who earned charms in nineteen ninety-six."

"I'd appreciate that."

"I don't suppose you remember anyone with a charm bracelet with items such as a shoe, a movie reel, and an ice cream cone?" I asked.

She shook her head. "No. I'm afraid I can't help you with that. While we had quite a few women who worked hard to earn the charm, I can't say that I remember seeing any of them actually wearing a charm bracelet."

After sharing my email address with Kendra, we thanked the woman for her help and then headed out to have lunch. I'd mentioned that I planned to head over to the high school at three to speak to Greta

Barber, and Jemma and Josie had volunteered to go with me since both women knew her from volunteer duties in the past.

"So have either of you heard any more about the missing teens?" I asked Jemma and Josie after we settled in at the restaurant.

"Not really," Josie answered. "I do know that they haven't been found, and I heard that the cops are stumped. No one claims to have seen anything, and the police were unable to find evidence of a motive when they searched their rooms and school lockers. The families have been interviewed, friends have been questioned, and the boy's usual hangouts searched, but so far, it looks like the three missing boys simply vanished."

"Have any of the parents have received a ransom demand or anything like that?" I asked.

"No," Josie answered. "No one has heard a thing. I think everyone is getting pretty frustrated, but at least so far, no bodies have been found, which means the potential exists for them to be alive."

"I wonder if there is anything we can do to help without stepping on Deputy Todd's toes," I said.

"I don't know. Maybe we should check in with Parker. It's her job to stay on top of things like this, and we all know that Parker is really good at her job."

Jemma called Parker, who informed Jemma that she had a meeting with her boss in an hour, but wondered if we might want to meet after work. Jemma and Josie were free, so we arranged to meet

Parker at Jemma and Josie's cottage at five-thirty. Josie professed a craving for steak and salad, so the roommates made up a list and planned to stop at the store after we spoke to Greta.

By the time we made it over to the high school, classes were just letting out. The high school I had attended was pretty industrial looking with long buildings sprayed with tan-colored paint, but Gooseberry Bay High, with its location up on a hill overlooking the bay, was actually quite charming.

"Josie, Jemma. What brings you to the high school today?" the woman in the theater asked.

"Greta, this is our friend, Ainsley, and she's helping a woman track down the owner of a charm bracelet," Josie explained. "One of the charms is a movie reel, and we thought that might represent the Movies on the Beach event we have here every summer."

"So you think the charms on the bracelet are clues to solving your little mystery," Greta stated, looking in my direction.

"We aren't sure, but we hope that by putting together the clues provided by the charms, we'll be able to figure this out," I answered.

"Even if the movie reel is meant to commemorate the Movies on the Beach event, we aren't sure what that tells us," Josie said.

"It occurred to Ainsley that perhaps the woman who owned the bracelet was a volunteer," Jemma added.

"If this woman would have been a volunteer, when would she have volunteered?" Greta asked.

"We think it would have been the summer of nineteen ninety-six," I answered.

"That's a long way back to remember something like who volunteered for movie detail that year," Greta pointed out.

"It is," I acknowledged. "I hoped that perhaps you kept records of some sort."

Greta paused to consider this. "We do have a party at the end of each season. It's a potluck sort of dinner, and all the volunteers bring a food item to share. I'm not sure if I kept the signup sheet, but I may have it on my computer. All the volunteers make a point to attend the party, so chances are if your charm lady was a volunteer, her name would be on the list."

"Does the list contain both first and last names?" I asked.

"First only, but if you find someone who seems to fit your parameters, I can usually remember last names. A lot of my volunteers help out year after year. Most are like family to me."

Jemma, Josie, and I thanked Greta after each of us volunteered to help out with the movie event this year. Greta promised to go through her files when she got home, and if she had the party attendee list from that year, she promised to email it to me."

"Volunteering for movie night actually sounds like a lot of fun," I said as we headed back to the peninsula after stopping at the store to pick up the items Josie wanted for dinner.

"It is fun," Josie offered. "I haven't done it the last few years, but I have helped out a time or two in the past. The only negative is that if you work the snack bar, you miss the movie. I always try to get the movie lineup ahead of time and volunteer for snack bar duty on the nights the movie they're playing is one I don't mind missing."

"I guess it would be hard to both sell snacks and watch the movie. Still, I think just being out under the stars with friends from the community on a warm summer night would be pretty awesome whether I had a chance to watch the movie or not."

"It is a good time to pick up some local gossip," Josie agreed.

When we got back to the peninsula, I headed to my cottage to take the dogs out for a short walk, promising Josie and Jemma that the dogs and I would be by in thirty minutes. Josie wanted to put together some appetizers, and Jemma had a couple calls to return. It was nice to have close friends who were willing to share their everyday moments. I supposed that without them, life out here on the peninsula might get pretty lonely.

By the time I'd made it to Josie and Jemma's cottage, Parker had arrived. We all gathered on the deck with wine and appetizers while Kai and Kallie played nearby with Stefan and Damon. Josie had missed some of the information Jemma and I had learned Monday, so Parker agreed to start at the beginning.

"Here's what I know," Parker said. "There are three boys, all fifteen, all Gooseberry High students, who went missing between Saturday and Monday. Zane Maddox was reported missing first. He left his house Sunday in the late afternoon to go paddleboarding. Since Zane lives near a narrow inlet that opens into the bay, he left his house on foot, planning to enter the water near his home and then paddle out to the bay. According to Zane's mother, when Zane left the house, he was in one of his moods, so when he didn't come home, she just figured he crashed with one of the friends he'd been planning to meet. When he didn't show up at school the following day, she was worried, and when his paddleboard was found floating in the bay, feelings of concern quickly segued into feelings of terror."

Parker took a breath and then continued. I figured we'd let her say what she had on her mind and then ask questions if there were aspects we felt needed clarification.

"Kalen West wasn't reported missing until after Zane's paddleboard was found, but it looks as if he might actually have been the first teen to go missing. Kalen's mother shared that things at home have been tense. Kalen's parents decided to split up, and Kalen hasn't taken that well. In fact, his mother reported that he has barely been tolerable to live with. When he left the house Saturday on the old dirt bike he bought a while back, he mumbled something about crashing with friends and not coming home that night.

When Kalen didn't show up Saturday night, his mother was unconcerned. When he didn't show up Sunday, she figured he was still in one of his moods and would get himself to school. When Kalen's mother heard about Zane, she called the school, only to discover that he'd never shown up that morning. At that point, Kalen's mother filed a missing persons report. Then Trevor Wilson turned up missing Monday as well. He was last seen leaving the school on his bicycle at three o'clock. He was grounded, so his instructions were to go straight home, but he never made it home."

"So if the three boys weren't friends, what links them?" I asked. "Other than being the same age and attending the same high school."

"Deputy Todd isn't sure at this point," Parker said. "He did say that all three boys had been exhibiting deviant behavior in the weeks leading up to their disappearance, but they were fifteen-year-old boys. I suppose deviant behavior comes with the territory."

"Does Todd have any actual clues?" Josie asked.

"Deputy Todd has the paddleboard Zane left the house with. It's not much of a clue, but it's something. We don't know when the paddleboard was placed into the water, so we don't know if Zane actually did head to the water to meet friends Saturday or if he just used the idea of paddleboarding to get away from the house."

"And Kalen's dirt bike?" I asked.

"It was parked at that lot across from the marina. Todd had it impounded."

"And Todd didn't find friends of any of the boys who might have seen them?" Josie asked.

"No. Zane and Kalen left home on a weekend of their own free will and presumably headed out to meet up with friends, but never did. Deputy Todd sees their disappearance as differing from Trevor's since Trevor hadn't been heading out but heading home when he went missing. At one point, Deputy Todd thought that maybe Zane and Kalen had simply gone off somewhere together."

"Are Zane and Kalen friends?" I asked. I'd asked Jemma this before but figured it would be good to get a different perspective.

"Not really," Parker answered. "At least not anymore. Zane is a jock. He plays all the sports and is super popular, so he tends to hang out with the popular crowd. Kalen used to be athletic, but after his parents split up, he began to cut practice in favor of hanging out with a group of kids who are into cars and street racing."

"And Trevor?" I asked.

"I actually spoke to Trevor's counselor today," Parker said. "She's a friend of mine and told me that Trevor is really smart and that his math, science, and computer skills are off the chart, although academically, he's been struggling lately. Not because he's unable to do the work, but because he's basically stopped turning anything in. My friend said that, in her opinion, Trevor is having a hard time balancing his intellectual needs with his social needs."

"So it's unlikely the three hung out with the same crowd," I said.

"Very unlikely," Parker agreed.

"Given the timeline, I think we need to assume that all three boys are missing for the same reason," I said. "They all could have been kidnapped, which I hope isn't what is going on, but does seem possible given the fact they're the same age."

"What does Deputy Todd think happened?" Josie asked.

"At this point, he's going with the kidnapping theory," Parker said. "I guess I get that. If they have been detained by someone, then they are probably in real danger, and finding them is critical, so that's where he's focusing his attention at the moment."

"Is there anything we can do to help?" I asked.

Parker frowned. "I'm not sure. I guess it wouldn't hurt if we poked around a bit. Maybe even talked to some of the boy's friends. If they did take off, it's possible that the boy's friends lied when they were interviewed by the police." Parker got up to take a call. "Let me poke around a bit, and I'll let the three of you know if there's something you can do."

Apparently, one of Parker's confidential informants had something for her, so she left to meet up with her CI and then head home. After she left, Jemma, Josie, and I grilled our steaks. Once we'd eaten, we sat down to compare the list of runners

Jemma had previously pulled up with the list of reading champions Kendra had emailed to me.

"There are seven names that overlap the two lists," Jemma said. "I recognize two of the seven. Both Heidi Vargas and Olive Brown live in town. I guess we can start by talking to them. Even if the bracelet doesn't belong to either of them, they may recognize it."

"Do you have their phone numbers?" I asked.

"I can get them. I'll try to get contact information for the five names I don't recognize as well. Do you want to meet up in the morning to go over things?"

"I do," I answered.

"I'm afraid I have to work," Josie said. "I have an early shift, so I'll get off early. If there's anything interesting going on, I can jump in then."

"What time should I come over?" I asked Jemma.

"Actually, maybe mid-morning. I really should check in with work first thing."

"Is ten-thirty okay?"

"That's perfect," Jemma agreed.

After I got back to my cottage, I called my client with an update. She was thrilled with the progress I'd already made. She'd spent the day walking up and down the boardwalk, showing the bracelet to vendors who worked the area, but so far, she hadn't found anyone who remembered someone from twenty-five years ago wearing anything like it.

It wasn't surprising no one remembered anything. There were a few cart vendors who'd been around back then, but by and large, the group of men and women who worked the boardwalk tended to have a large turnover. The work was physical, for one thing. Since you couldn't simply lock up your wares at the end of each day, the inventory displayed had to be packed up each night and then brought out again each morning. It was a cycle that most folks tired of after a few years, hence the turnover.

After I'd washed up and put on my pajamas, I opened one of the boxes that Warren had sent me and began to sort through it. Looking at the old photos and mementos was emotionally draining, but it was helping me to get to know the couple who'd bore me. My father had a crooked smile and tended to wear the most out-of-date argyle sweaters I'd ever seen. I really had no idea what was in style in Italy during the nineties, but they were definitely out of date here in the States now.

My mother was beautiful, petite, and blond. She had a soft smile in comparison to my father's wide grin. She tended to prefer stylish yet conservative clothes. I supposed that made sense given her position in society, but hadn't the woman owned a single pair of blue jeans?

The longer I looked at the photos, the more the couple, who at one point must have meant the world to me, began to feel real. It was odd to know that we'd been a family. It felt strange knowing that I'd been a completely different person for the first three years of my life than I'd been for the next twenty-five years. I felt like I should feel something when I looked at photos of Avery and me as babies. I did feel a bit of a connection toward Avery, but when I looked at photos of myself, I felt like I was looking at a stranger. I thought back to my dad, the man who'd raised me. I could remember his crooked grin and sense of humor that was often offbeat. I remembered the way he'd roll the ice around in his whisky for a good minute before taking a single sip, and I also remembered the strong arms that held me tight when life proved to be cruel and my heart or spirit was harmed in some way.

My dad was real to me when I thought of him, but when I looked at Arthur and Adora, they mostly felt like strangers. I wondered if that would ever change. I supposed that even if I ended up finding all my answers, I could never really know them. Not really. Not the way I'd known the cop who'd raised me. It was sad that my parents would always be a mystery to me, but I supposed that given their deaths when I was so young, that inevitable fact had been sealed early on. Even if Marilee hadn't taken Avery and me away, even if we'd stayed in our childhood home, our memories of the man and woman who'd bore us would have been limited to what others shared rather than what we'd experienced.

Setting the box aside, I headed into the bedroom. It was late, and I was tired but also discontent. I really wanted to feel something when I looked at the photo of my mother. Anything. Maybe if I fell asleep picturing my mother's face, I'd be able to remember something, even if that memory did exist only in my dream space.

Chapter 7

I woke early Thursday and decided to head out for a long run with the dogs. I wasn't sure how my day was going to work out, and I suspected that the dogs might end up being alone for much of the day. Not that they'd mind. Not really. Both Kai and Kallie tended to sleep a lot, and as long as they had a good long walk in the morning, they were usually good for the rest of the day.

As I ran along the bay trail, I thought about my plans for the day. I'd meet with Jemma this morning, and I supposed that what I did next depended on the outcome of that conversation. If she was able to put together some clues relating to the charm bracelet, I supposed I'd spend the rest of the day tracking down those clues. Ellery was leaving town Sunday, and I really hoped that we would have found an answer before she left if there was an answer to be found.

As I climbed up onto the point, I thought about the charms. The shoe and the book seemed to have offered us the best chances to actually track down the person who at one point had owned the charms. Jemma had said there were seven names that she found on both lists. Seven was actually a reasonable number of people to track down and speak to. When Ellery had come to me with her quest, I'd wanted to help if I could, but to be honest, I hadn't held a lot of hope that we'd actually be successful, but now it seemed that we might come out of this investigation with a name. What she did with that name would be up to her.

I really thought that the lists we had would give us our answer, but if not we'd need to turn our attention to the remaining charms. As we'd speculated the previous evening, I was pretty sure that the Ferris wheel charm had most likely been a token from the annual carnival. I wasn't sure what more we could do with that clue. The carnival wasn't even in town, so trying to find employees who were around back then probably wasn't a realistic goal.

And then there was the ice cream cone charm. We all agreed that the charm was too general to be of much use unless we could tie it to a specific ice cream shop. It was a long shot, but I supposed if we were able to do that and the ice cream shop was still around, it might lead us to someone who would remember the bracelet.

The rose, like the ice cream cone, seemed too general to provide much information. We'd discussed that the rose charm might lead to a florist, although there were other possibilities as well. There were lovely gardens in the area and when we'd visited the museum, I noticed that rose bushes were planted along the building. I supposed we could look around for other gardens, or perhaps a hothouse or nursery was the link we needed to find.

And then there was the ship. It could represent any boat or even the ferry, I supposed, but the charm looked more like a Navy ship. Could Ellery's father have been in the Navy? Perhaps her mother had entered into a summer romance with a boy she'd met in Gooseberry Bay only to find that he'd shipped out for a tour overseas at the end of their time together. I had no idea how to follow up on a theory such as that since we didn't have a name for either parent. Still, an explanation that included a summer love with a military man might explain why Ellery's mother felt she was unable to keep her.

After I'd turned around at the fence and started back toward my cottage, I let my mind drift to the missing boys. I really hoped that there was news that all the boys had been found safe by the time I checked in with Jemma. I knew that the longer they were missing, the less likely it was that they'd be found alive. I had no idea how I could help, and I certainly hadn't been asked to, but the knot in my gut that wouldn't quite let me walk away was getting more intense with each day that passed without a resolution.

After I returned to the cottage, I fed the dogs, gave them fresh water, showered and dressed, and then headed to meet with Jemma. When I arrived, she opened the door and motioned me in, although I could see she was on the phone.

"Yes. I understand. I'll get on it right away," Jemma said to whomever she was talking to. "It won't be a problem. Look for it in three or four hours." With that, she hung up and looked at me. "I'm sorry. That was my boss. He needs a last-minute adjustment to some code I wrote months ago. I'm afraid I won't be able to go with you to speak to the women on the list we've come up with."

"That's no problem. Is everything okay at work?"

She sighed. "Yeah. It's fine. Even though I worked while I was away, I guess being gone for a month put me behind more than I thought. The changes my boss is looking for aren't all that complicated. I can probably knock them out in a few hours, but he does want them today." She handed me a piece of paper. "These are the phone numbers for the two women whose names I recognized from the list. Heidi Vargas works at Pretty in Pink, that cute little boutique on Seventh Street with the pink and black sign. I already called her and briefly explained what we were after. She said she'd be happy to talk to us if we wanted to stop in. I'll text her and let her know you're coming alone if you want to speak to her."

"I'd like to speak to her. If she did the Bay to Boardwalk Run and Brewster's Books Reading

Challenge, she might know the woman we're looking for."

"Maybe. Heidi is around fifty-five, I'd guess. Since she was already married with children during the summer of ninety-six, she may not have been in the same peer group as the mother of your client. That's assuming that your client is even on the right track and the woman who owned the bracelet actually was her biological mother, and we're correct in our assumption that your client's biological mother was actually younger than twenty-two at the time of your client's birth. At this point, we're operating on a lot of guesswork that we have no way of verifying."

"Yeah. There really aren't many, if any, known facts at this point, but I think it's definitely worth having a chat with Heidi."

"I thought you could take both lists along with you and ask her about some of the other names as well if she isn't too busy."

"Okay. I can do that. Did you also speak to Olive Brown?"

"I did. Olive works at the mini-mart down near the marina. She's willing to speak to us too, although she sounded less certain that she'd remember anything. She was just seventeen during the summer of ninety-six, which in my opinion, most likely puts her closer in age to the owner of the charm bracelet, so maybe something will come to her."

"Okay, thanks," I said after accepting the lists and slipping them into my pocket. "Good luck with your work stuff today."

"Thanks. Call me later," Jemma said. "I'm interested in how everything works out."

"I will. And thanks again."

Deciding to head to Pretty in Pink and speak to Heidi first, I checked on the dogs one more time and then headed toward the parking area. Pretty in Pink was a cute boutique with light pink walls and black accents, providing a chic and sophisticated feel. I'd thought about checking the place out a few times in the past when I'd driven by, but, so far, I never had.

"Heidi Vargas?" I asked after entering the shop.

"You must be Ainsley."

"I am. I appreciate you taking the time to meet with me."

"Nineteen ninety-six was a long time ago, but if there is anything I can do to help you find the woman you're looking for, I'm happy to help."

I quickly explained why I was interested in women who'd participated in the Bay to Boardwalk Run and Brewster's Books Reading Challenge in nineteen ninety-six and then showed her the photos of the charms.

"I can't say that I remember anyone wearing a bracelet such as this. There was a group of us who earned book charms for meeting the top goal. I didn't even have a bracelet and just tossed my charm into a drawer. I suspect that the majority of winners from that group did the same."

"Jemma identified seven names that were on both the list from the run and the list from the reading challenge. I wondered if you'd take a look at the list and see if you recognize any of the names."

"I'd be happy to." She held out her hand, and I handed her both lists. The seven names that showed up on both lists had been highlighted. "I see you have my name highlighted as well as Olive Brown's. Have you spoken to Olive?"

"I'm planning to head there next."

She seemed satisfied with that and looked back down at the lists. "Nancy Bayberry is listed as having participated in the run and completing the reading challenge." Heidi looked up. "Nancy moved away at least a decade ago, but we knew each other when she lived here. She was married to a man named Ted in nineteen ninety-six. They had three sons. I'm fairly certain that she isn't the person you're looking for if the person you hope to find would have been pregnant in nineteen ninety-six."

"Okay, thank you. That helps. Now I just have four names on the list who we've yet to track down. Caroline Grant, Brandy Heffner, Rosalie Watts, and Naomi Potter. Do any of those names ring a bell?"

She slowly shook her head. "No. I can't say that any of those names sound familiar. You need to keep in mind that while the reading challenge was mainly local, folks came from all around to do the run. If the woman you're looking for simply purchased or was gifted the book charm from a friend who completed the challenge, she may not have even lived in the area."

"I suppose that's a possibility, but the fact that the woman who abandoned her baby in a church left the bracelet with the infant leads me to believe the bracelet meant a lot to her. I can't see that person simply buying or accepting charms that represent someone else's accomplishments."

"I suppose that's true." Heidi looked up when the bell over the door rang. "Silvia," she greeted a tall thin woman who looked to be around fifty. "I have the alterations done on the dress you bought earlier in the week."

"That's perfect. I'm heading out of town for a conference tomorrow and really wanted to take it with me."

Heidi turned to me. "Silvia Cornwall, this is Ainsley Holloway. Ainsley is a private investigator currently trying to track down the owner of a charm bracelet."

"Nice to meet you," I replied.

"Silvia is a counselor at the high school. I think she was here in nineteen ninety-six."

Silvia nodded. "I started in the counseling department for Gooseberry High in ninety-four. Do you think you're looking for a student?"

"I'm not sure." I quickly shared the story of the abandoned baby who was now an adult and had hired me to track down the owner of the bracelet, who she believed would turn out to be her biological mother, while Heidi went into the back to fetch the dress.

"That's both a sad and interesting story. I'm not sure a bracelet like that is the sort of thing that would be worn by a high school student in the mid-nineties, and I don't remember any students being pregnant. I'm happy to take a look at your lists, however, if you think I might be able to help."

"I'd appreciate that." I handed her the lists.

She furrowed her brow as she looked at the highlighted names. "I do recognize a lot of names on both these lists, but as for the four names on both lists you've yet to track down, I'm afraid none seem familiar. I see that one of the charms is an ice cream cone. There was a girl named Naomi who worked at Bayside Ice Cream around the time you are researching. I don't know her last name."

"Does she still live in town?"

"No. I think Naomi was just here for the summer. There was a group of kids here for the summer. They stayed in those cabins over off Sunset Beach."

"Kids?" I asked.

"I guess they weren't kids, but they were young. If I had to guess, the lot of them fell into the eighteen to twenty age range. The cabins cater to folks who are in the area looking for summer jobs."

"Is Bayside Ice Cream still around?" I asked, not recognizing the name.

"Actually, no. Not really. Bayside Ice Cream was owned by a woman who retired a decade ago and moved to Arizona. She sold the place to a man named Tony Trauner. He still owns the place. If the Naomi on this list is the same Naomi who worked for Bayside Ice Cream, Tony may be able to help you. Tony started off working for Bayside before buying the place and changing the name to Scoops and Sprinkles."

I smiled at the woman as she handed my lists back to me. "I appreciate your help. Every little clue helps."

"Happy to do what I can." She paused and then continued. "I guess you must have heard about the missing boys."

I nodded. "Yes, I'm afraid I have. I guess if you work at the high school, you must know them."

"I know them well," she confirmed. "All the missing boys are from families who've lived in the area for quite some time. I just can't imagine what's going on. First, there are all the changes, and then the boys go missing."

"Changes?"

"Personality changes." She leaned in a bit as if to share a secret. "I know that most folks simply chalk up the fact that the boys seemed to have been going through a rebellious stage to hormones and naturally occurring teen angst, and I suppose to a point, that might be true, but I feel like there was more to it. I'm not sure what exactly. It almost seemed as if someone got into the heads of these boys and convinced them that to truly be happy, they needed to defy their parents and make their own way."

"I suppose that pulling away from parental influence is natural for fifteen-year-olds in general."

"Yes, that is true. I guess I just noticed some commonalities between the three boys that I found odd."

"Commonalities?"

"It started with Kalen. Kalen was always a nice kid, but he took it hard when his parents decided to split up. He dropped out of the sports teams he played on and began cutting classes. He started hanging out with a different group of kids than he'd grown up with. I was actually a bit surprised by how hard he was taking things since Kalen was the independent sort even before the breakup. After his dad left, he pretty much decided he was going to make his own decisions in life and began doing just that. Of course, not all the decisions he made were good decisions, so he ended up in my office most weeks for one reason or another."

"So when a student gets into trouble, are they sent to talk to you?" I asked.

"Sometimes. It depends on the transgression and the motive behind the bad behavior, but yes, when a student is struggling, it's not uncommon for them to be sent to talk to me. Anyway, like I said, Kalen had been a regular visitor in my office by the time Zane began coming around almost as often. I knew that Zane and his father hadn't been getting along. Zane's dad has always been harsh in his approach to child-rearing. I'm sure Zane never had it easy, but when he was younger, Zane had apparently figured out how to manage his father by avoiding certain actions, so it wasn't too much of a problem. During the last weeks before he went missing, however, something changed. Instead of avoiding behavior that would set his dad off, Zane seemed to almost be egging him on by doing exactly the opposite of what he demanded."

"Okay, so we have two teenage boys who are angry at their parents and begin to lash out. You mentioned commonalities."

She nodded. "I first noticed Kalen using terms like personal power and one life. It sort of sounded like he had gotten ahold of a motivational handbook of some sort. It's not unusual for kids around that age to begin to look inward for meaning, so it wouldn't be outside the realm of possibility that Kalen had begun to think about who he was as an individual. I suspected at the time that the divorce had triggered that introspection. He went from being a kid who probably felt safe in an intact family to one who felt threatened when that family imploded."

"I guess that makes sense. And Zane?"

"Zane's life situation hadn't changed the way Kalen's had, although his sister did go off to college this past fall, and I think that up to that point, she served as sort of an anchor for him. Their father is strict and, at times, cruel in his approach to parenting. I think the two children banded together to get through things. Zane seemed to be the sort of kid who'd learned to adapt to his situation, but after his sister left, he began to push back, and his mother told me that she could feel him pulling away. What I found most interesting was that when Zane talked about some of the decisions he'd made, he also used the terms personal power and one life."

"The exact same terms?" I asked.

She nodded. "The exact same terms. The use of the words *personal power* can be found in a lot of self-help and personal empowerment type books, but the term *one life* seems unique. Unfortunately, I didn't really pick up on it until I went back through my notes after the boys went missing."

"And Trevor?" I asked.

"Trevor is a smart kid. Brilliant, in fact. Lately, however, he's had a hard time in school. It's not because he can't do the work, but because he's refusing to participate. I spoke to Trevor's parents about a private school for gifted students, but they didn't want to move, and they didn't want to send him off to board. Trevor is a good kid with a superior mind, but he's also interested in doing what he wants to do. Still, he does generally seem to respect his parents."

"So how does he fit in with the others?" I asked.

"I guess I should have said that Trevor has been a good kid who has generally respected his parents until recently. That all seemed to change a month or so ago when Trevor got it into his head that he was going to drop out of school and start his own video game company."

I cringed. I hated to see a smart kid give up on having a higher education.

"Of course, given his age, his parents were against the idea, but it seemed that Trevor had made up his mind, so he began cutting classes. I worked with his parents to find a solution to the problem, but short of following Trevor from class to class, there was little they could do to keep him in school. Still, they tried. They all met with me. They restricted his privileges when he cut classes and provided rewards when he attended. They did what they could, but Trevor had decided that he was old enough to make his own choices and was determined to do just that."

"Let me guess. During your sessions, Trevor used terms such as personal power and one life."

She nodded. "Those exact terms. Again, I wish I would have honed in on this as being a problem before the boys went missing, but I guess I was more concerned about finding a solution to the problem than I was in identifying the reason the problem existed in the first place."

"So what do you think it means that all three missing kids suddenly started using these exact terms about the same time they began to act out?"

Heidi returned with the dress and headed to the register to ring up the charge for the alterations.

"I think that all three boys somehow came into contact with the same book or possibly the same person," Silvia answered. "I think that the terms personal power and one life are concepts they were exposed to, and I think that all three were vulnerable enough to be drawn in."

I narrowed my gaze. "So what does that mean? How would something like that lead to their disappearance?"

"I'm hoping this means that the boys formed a support group or secret society of some sort based on this book or motivational speaker. I'm hoping the boys simply took off to explore the concept of personal power and will eventually show up."

I followed Silvia to the cash register.

"I hope that is true as well." I paused while she paid for her alterations. "Do you think they will show up on their own?"

She shrugged. "I can't be sure, but I think they might."

After Sylvia left, I headed to Scoops and Sprinkles to talk to Tony Trauner. I had to admit that I was worried about the three missing boys, but I didn't think I knew enough about any of the boys to actually be of help in finding them. Besides, Ellery was my client. She was counting on me to help her track down the owner of the charm bracelet, and that was exactly what I planned to do.

Chapter 8

Tony Trauner wasn't in when I stopped by the ice cream shop. The woman working the counter told me that he'd be in on Saturday afternoon, so I told her I'd check back then. I had the kiddie carnival that morning, but I figured that if I hadn't already solved the mystery of the charm bracelet by that point, I could stop in after my shift at the park.

Deciding to swing by the mini-mart where Olive worked while I was in town, I changed direction and headed toward the water. When I arrived, a woman who looked to be the right age to be Olive was ringing up an order, so I decided to wait. The view of the water out the front window of the little store was exceptional. I supposed there were worse places to work.

"Olive?" I asked after her customer left.

She frowned. "I'm sorry. Do I know you?"

"My name is Ainsley Holloway."

Her frown changed to a smile. "Of course. You're Jemma's friend." She looked around. "Is she here?"

"No. Jemma ended up with a project for work, so I came on my own. I hope that's okay."

"It's fine. Jemma told me that you have some photos you'd like me to look at."

I nodded and handed her the stack of photos I'd printed of the bracelet and the individual charms. "I'm looking for the woman who may have owned this bracelet back in nineteen ninety-six. So far, we've been able to identify the book as the charm given to those who reached the highest level of the reading challenge Brewster's Books sponsored, and the shoe as representing the Bay to Boardwalk Run. I have lists of the individuals who participated in the run that year and the individuals who received the book charm." I set both lists on the counter. "So far, I've spoken to Heidi Vargas, who remembered Nancy Bayberry. She mentioned that Nancy has since moved away, but she's pretty certain that Nancy isn't the one we're looking for."

"Jemma mentioned something about a baby."

"Yes. My client was left in a church as an infant in nineteen ninety-seven. The charm bracelet in the photo was left with her. It's her belief that the bracelet belonged to her biological mother. She'd like to track her down and is hoping we'll be able to identify her with the clues provided."

She looked down at the lists. "In addition to Heidi, Nancy, and me, you have Caroline Grant, Brandy Heffner, Rosalie Watts, and Naomi Potter highlighted."

"Yes. All seven names were on the list for the run, and the list Kendra Hart provided for the reading challenge."

"I was just seventeen in nineteen ninety-six, so I wasn't paying a lot of attention to who was doing what, but I do remember Brandy Heffner. She was my age and got married a few years later. She did have children, but not until after she married, and I don't remember her being pregnant or leaving town for an extended period before that, so I sort of doubt that she's your baby mama. She still lives in Gooseberry Bay, however, so I guess you can ask her about it."

I smiled. "Do you know how I can get ahold of Brandy?"

She nodded. "Her name is Brandy Winfield now. She's married to Matt Winfield. Matt is a licensed contractor, and Brandy takes care of the clerical stuff for his business. I don't have her phone number offhand, but if you look up Winfield Construction, you should be able to track her down."

"Thank you so much. I appreciate the help. Is there anything else you can tell me about either the names on the list or the charms?"

She took a second look at the photos. "The ship looks like one of those Navy ships that are sometimes seen in the Sound. There's a shipyard in Bremerton, and it's not unusual for Gooseberry Bay to play host to a slew of Navy boys on leave. I wonder if the ship is included to represent the baby's father."

"I actually did think of that. It occurred to me that Ellery's biological mother could have met her biological father here over the summer. If he shipped out shortly after, he might not have known about the baby. If the mother was young, possibly even a teenager, she may have felt unequipped to care for a baby on her own, so she left her in the church."

"Your theory makes sense up to a point, but if this young girl did end up pregnant and alone, why didn't she put the baby up for adoption? There are a lot of folks looking for babies. She didn't need to abandon her."

Olive had a point. A good point. If Ellery's biological mother was alone and afraid, why not make arrangements for her baby before she was born? Why would she leave her naked in a blanket the way she had?

I thanked Olive for the information she'd provided and then got to work looking up a number for Winfield Construction. It was already Thursday, and I really did hope to have this mystery wrapped up this week. After I located the number and called the business office, I explained to Brandy who I was and what I was after, and she invited me to come by her home. As would be expected for a contractor, the Winfield home was absolutely stunning.

"Your house is gorgeous," I said after the perky brunette invited me in.

"Thanks. Matt and I took our time and made sure the home we built would be exactly what we wanted and needed for our growing family." She motioned with her hand. "Please, do come in, and we'll have a chat."

After she showed me to the sunroom and offered me a seat, she asked if I wanted iced tea. When I declined, she asked what sort of information I was looking for. I share the story of my client and her unconventional birth, and then I explained how my client suspected the bracelet would help her find her biological mother and her desire to do so.

"Well, I can start off by letting you know that I didn't have a child out of wedlock, nor did I abandon a child in a church, so you can cross my name off the list." She paused to really look over the remaining names. "Caroline Grant was a summer resident back in the nineties. Her family owned a vacation house in the area, and Caroline and her mother and brothers would come for a couple months every summer. I won't say we were super close, but we did have interests in common. We both liked to run, and we both liked to read. We also both volunteered for several different events. The carnival and movie night and a few others."

It sounded as if Carolyn checked quite a few boxes if she was involved in both the Bay to Boardwalk Run and Brewster's Books Reading Challenge, and she volunteered for the movie and even the carnival. "So Carolyn would come for a couple months and then go home?" I asked.

"Yes. Carolyn's family lived in Seattle."

"Do you remember seeing Carolyn during the summer of nineteen ninety-six?"

"Sure. Caroline was going to be a senior the following year, and so was I. We were both excited about what the future might bring and sad to see our high school years coming to an end."

"Did you see her in the summer of nineteen ninety-seven?"

She slowly shook her head. "No. I don't think she came to Gooseberry Bay that year. I seem to remember something about a graduation trip with some friends."

"And after that?"

"I do remember running into her a few times during the next years. Carolyn never came back for the whole summer like she had when she was a kid, but her parents still owned the vacation house, so she came for long weekends every now and then." She paused and then continued. "I think the family sold the house after their youngest son graduated a few years later."

The baby was abandoned in a church just north of Seattle. It was beginning to look as if Carolyn might be the woman we were looking for. Brandy had no idea how to get ahold of her at this point, and she had no idea if she'd married and changed her last name. Brandy suggested I speak to a woman named Valerie Craig, who still lived in the area. According to Brandy, Valerie had been closer to Carolyn than she'd been during their teen years and thus was more apt to have kept in touch with her after she graduated from high school. Brandy didn't have contact information for Valerie but suggested that I look her up through the high school alumni association. Apparently, Valerie was active in high school sports as a booster. I thought of Silvia, who worked at the high school and decided to start with her. If she knew how to get ahold of Valerie, that seemed to be the easiest way to go about contacting the woman.

As it turned out, Silvia did have a phone number for Valerie, so I called and asked Valerie if we could chat. She worked at the local sewing and quilting store. She informed me that she'd be there until three, and if I wanted to speak to her, I could show up there at any point until she was off for the day.

"Yes, I knew Caroline fairly well back in the nineties," Valerie confirmed after I'd filled her in on the reason for my questions. "You indicated that Brandy already explained that she was a summer-only resident. Her family lived in Seattle but owned a home in the area. Caroline's mother and brothers came to Gooseberry Bay every summer from about the time school let out until a couple weeks before they went back for the fall semester. During the months they were here in town, Caroline and I hung out almost every day."

"Brandy mentioned that Caroline ran in the same run she had and managed to meet the top goal presented by Brewster's Books for the reading challenge."

"That's right. Caroline was really into running and reading. And she was fast. I think she actually won the Bay to Boardwalk Run for her age group that last year she was here before graduation."

"Wow. That's wonderful. There were a lot of entrants."

"It used to be a really popular event. Folks came from all over the state."

"Brandy mentioned that Caroline also enjoyed volunteering for local events such as the movie night and the carnival."

"We both did. If I'm perfectly honest, I wasn't really into running or reading, but I did like to help out, so Caroline and I pitched in where we could. Of course, that final summer, Caroline met Justin, and the time the two of us spent together was greatly diminished."

"Justin?"

"Some preppy college boy who blew in on his daddy's yacht and stayed for several weeks."

It sounded as if Valerie was jealous of Justin even now. "So, how did Caroline and Justin meet?"

"Caroline was working the ice cream booth at the carnival, and Justin came by with a couple of his preppy friends. I'm not sure what Caroline said to him, but it seemed that he was instantly smitten. Once Caroline met Justin, she spent more of her time with him than she did with me. If you're wondering if that made me angry, yes, it did. I really looked forward to Caroline's visits each summer, and I sensed that once we both graduated, things would probably never be the same between us. I really wanted that last summer together to be our epic summer, but instead of the long hot days being all about us, it ended up being all about Caroline and Justin."

"Did the relationship last?" I wondered.

"No. A few weeks before Caroline was supposed to go back to Seattle, Justin blew out of town on that fancy yacht of his just as quietly as he blew in. Caroline and I were never as close as we had once been after that point. She was upset and looking to me for comfort, while I was just happy the guy had left."

"Brandy mentioned that Caroline came back to the island again a few times after that, although not for the summer."

"That's true. After Caroline and her family went back to Seattle at the end of that summer, I didn't see her for almost two years. Then when her youngest brother was in high school, they came a few times for long weekends. Eventually, they sold the house."

"Did you stay in touch with Caroline after that?" I asked.

"Not really. In fact, I totally lost track of Caroline until two years ago. She came to the island with her husband and children, and we ran into each other at a movie night. We exchanged emails and phone numbers. I send Caroline a note every now and again, and she sends photos of her kids from time to time."

"I'd love to speak to her about that summer. Do you think she would mind if you gave me her cell or email?"

Valerie paused. "I'm not sure. How about I take your information and pass it on to her. If she wants to talk to you, she can contact you."

"That seems fair," I agreed.

I left my contact information with Valerie, hoping that Caroline would call. It really did sound as if she might be the woman we were looking for.

Chapter 9

When I got back to my cottage and checked my emails, I noticed that I had one from Greta, with a signup sheet from the volunteer dinner held in nineteen ninety-six attached to it. I did a quick check and found that someone named Caroline and someone named Valerie had signed up to bring chips and dip. Since the list only provided first names, it didn't tell me a lot, but after speaking to Valerie, I was sure that Caroline was the woman I was looking for. Now I just had to wait and see if she called me. Waiting would be frustrating, but waiting was my only choice at the moment, so I changed into my running clothes and headed out with the dogs. Two runs in one day was a lot, so I decided to walk. In fact, a walk along the waterline so the dogs could splash around in the bay seemed like an outing they'd enjoy quite a lot.

As I walked along the beach, I thought about my client. I could really identify with someone looking for their roots and hoped our search would provide the answers she sought. It was an odd sort of feeling to not feel connected to the people who brought you into this world, and I was sure that Ellery must have questions for which she needed answers.

I paused when we came to the spot on the beach where the bay curved around to the north. I sat on a large rock and looked out across the vast expanse of icy clear water. It was a beautiful day – the sort of day that demanded that you stop and take a minute to appreciate its perfection. There hasn't been a single day that's gone by since I landed in Gooseberry Bay when I haven't stopped to marvel at the perfection of my life since arriving in town.

I was about to get up and head toward home when my phone buzzed. It was a number I didn't recognize, but I'd forwarded the landline at Ainsley Holloway Investigations to my cell, so I answered.

"Ainsley Holloway," I said after hitting the answer button.

"Ms. Holloway. My name is Cora Maddox. I wondered if you had a few minutes to speak to me."

"Cora Maddox? Are you Zane Maddox's sister?"

"I am," she confirmed. "I guess you've heard that Zane is missing."

"Yes, I did hear. I'm so very sorry. Has there been news?"

"No. Not a bit, and Zane has been missing four days." She paused, and I waited. "When they first found his paddleboard, I actually thought he might be dead. Zane and I are three years apart in age, so we haven't always been super close, but he's my brother, and I love him. When I heard they found his paddleboard floating in the lake, I was inconsolable."

"And now?" I wasn't sure why exactly, but I suspected there was an "and now" around the corner in this conversation.

"Now I believe Zane to be alive. Alive, but not necessarily okay. I heard all about you from a friend and would like to hire you to find my brother."

Okay, I had to admit that I hadn't been expecting that. "You want to hire me to find Zane?"

"Yes. That's what I just said. Deputy Todd is a buffoon. I've spoken to him five times in the past four days, and all he will tell me is that it looks as if Zane fell off his paddleboard and drowned. Drowned! Zane is an excellent swimmer. Even if he'd fallen into the water, he'd have found a way to survive. And then there's the fact that two other boys turned up missing at the same time. There is no way my brother simply fell off his paddleboard and drowned."

I found I had to agree with Cora. Given the fact that three boys went missing in three days, it seemed much more likely they were abducted.

"Are you in town?" I asked, remembering that the sister had been away at college.

"I just got into town last night. It took me a couple days to arrange for travel from the east coast, but I'm here now, and I plan to stay until Zane is home safe. So will you take the case?"

I really wasn't sure I'd have any more luck finding Zane, and hopefully, the others, than Deputy Todd had had. Cora wasn't wrong when she called the man a buffoon, but I didn't think he was naive enough to actually think that Zane had simply fallen and drowned, so chances were he'd just told Cora that to get her off his back.

"I'd like to speak to you in person before I commit to taking on the case. I can meet you in my office in an hour."

"I'll be there." With that, she hung up.

I hurried back to the cottage and changed out of my shorts and into a pair of slacks and a summery top, pulled on a pair of sandals, checked to make sure the dogs had food and water, and then headed back to town. I wasn't sure exactly what was going on, but three missing fifteen-year-olds, all from the same high school and all the product of a recent personality change, left no doubt in my mind that the three disappearances were linked in some way.

Cora was early and waiting for me when I arrived. I ushered her into my office, offered her coffee, and took out my notepad and pen so I could jot down thoughts that came to me as we chatted. I asked her a few questions about herself to break the ice and then jumped into the subject at hand.

"Zane was last seen by your mother late Sunday afternoon. He left the house with his blue paddleboard after mentioning that he planned to meet up with friends. He never returned home that evening and hasn't been seen or heard from since. His paddleboard was found floating in the bay Monday. Initially, it was assumed that he'd had an accident or possibly a run-in with sea life and was dead. Until the other boys turned up missing, that was a reasonable theory. Since that point, it's been determined that both Kalen West and Trevor Wilson are also missing. This leads me to believe that the three boys have either been abducted or simply took off together of their own accord. At this point, I don't have much of an opinion as to which theory might be the more accurate." I looked directly at Cora. "I guess the first thing I'd like to ask you is whether or not you have an opinion as to what might be going on."

She nodded. "I do have an opinion as to whether Zane was abducted or ran off." She took a breath and adjusted her position as if settling in for a long explanation. "Zane is three years younger than I am. I think I might have mentioned that before. Given the age gap and the fact that I was a girl and he was a boy, we weren't always super close growing up, but we did have a bond. A strong bond at times." She hesitated and then continued. "You see, our father can be a brusque and rigid man. I know he's considered to be a leader in the community, and I'm aware of the fact that most Gooseberry Bay citizens hold him in high esteem, but as a father, he's a tough man to love."

I quietly waited for her to continue.

"As the older sibling, I tried to smooth things over for Zane when I could. Our father is the sort of man who has very specific expectations for his son, and most of the time, when he was younger, Zane tried very hard to meet those expectations. Zane is an excellent athlete and a hard worker, so the majority of the time, he got on with Dad just fine, but no one can be perfect all the time, so there were times Zane failed, and our father made sure he was made aware of his displeasure."

"Was your father physical with Zane?" I had to ask.

"No. Dad's displeasure was communicated in the form of psychological torture. I can't really explain it, but our father has a way of making you feel like a bug who deserves nothing more than to be squashed beneath his feet. Dad was that way with me as well, but as the only boy, Zane had it worse. I tried to be there for Zane when Dad came down on him." She smiled. "Zane's room is next to mine. When Zane was seven, he went into our father's office looking for a toy he'd been unable to find. Dad has a strict rule that no one is to go into his office for any reason, but Zane really wanted this specific toy, so he snuck in, figuring he could look for the toy and then sneak back out before Dad noticed. Of course, our father notices everything, and he confronted Zane, who confessed to entering the room. Our father sentenced Zane to his room for three days with only bread and water to eat and drink."

"That's horrible."

"It was. I felt so bad for Zane. I knew his punishment wouldn't kill him, but it wasn't going to be pleasant either. I wanted to help, so I borrowed a small handsaw from a friend and cut a hole through the wall in my closet, which I knew was a shared wall to Zane's closet."

"So you could enter his room without your dad knowing."

"Exactly. We used that opening to go back and forth all the time when we were growing up. Dad rarely went into our rooms. He didn't clean or put laundry away, so he never found out about our secret passage. I think Mom knew, but she never let on."

"Okay. Go on. You and Zane were allies while growing up. How does this help us find him now?"

"I'm not exactly sure it will, but I thought it was important that you understand how hard it was for Zane when I left for college last fall. Zane can take care of himself now. It's been a long time since he was a terrified seven-year-old trying to figure out how to deal with an ogre of a father, but I think my leaving was hard on him all the same. Harder than I thought it would be. Not that he said as much. Zane wanted me to get out of that house, so he supported my leaving, but I did notice a personality change once I'd left. I'm not sure exactly how, but I believe that his disappearance is linked to the changes I've noticed when we've spoken lately."

Okay, the theme of personality change in all three boys had come up before. I picked up my pen and tapped it against the notebook on my desk. "Tell me about this personality change. What specifically did you notice?"

She shifted in her chair as if trying to find a comfortable position. "I was hesitant to go to college and leave Zane behind, but he assured me that he'd be fine, and at first, it seemed like he was. He made the varsity football team, which made our father happy. He was doing okay in school and staying out of trouble. I spoke to him every week at first and came home at Christmas. Things seemed good, so I began to relax. Our communications with each other significantly lessened after I returned to school after Christmas break. He was busy; I was busy. Life got in the way, and the weekly calls became more and more sporadic. Still, Zane seemed to be doing fine, and then about six weeks ago, he started making comments about meeting someone who was really helping him work through his issues with our father. At first, I didn't think anything about it. The things Zane said seemed to be positive and life-affirming. He talked about finding his own power and personal growth. He talked about figuring out what he wanted out of life instead of making every decision based on what he thought would lead to the least amount of resistance from our father. It sounded good to me. It sounded like he was growing up and taking charge of his own life. But then, Mom called me in tears a few weeks ago. Zane had quit the baseball team and was failing half his classes. The harder our father tried to bring him into line, the more he resisted. Mom told me that things were becoming tense. She was afraid that things would get physical. I told her I'd come home as soon as school let out for the summer, and I assured her that I planned to spend the entire summer in Gooseberry Bay. That seemed to help a bit. At least it helped her."

"So what are you saying?" I asked. "Do you think Zane simply took off?"

"No. I don't think Zane took off. If he had decided to run away, he would have let me know. He knew I'd be worried, and I really don't think he would intentionally do anything to cause me the amount of duress his disappearance has caused."

"Did Zane ever use the phrase *one life*?" I asked.

She frowned. "Actually, Zane did use that phrase when we last spoke. He said something about only having one life to live and making sure that the one life he had to live was a life of his choosing. Do you think that whatever sort of personal growth thing he was into is related to all of this?"

"Maybe. I spoke to a woman named Silvia Cromwell while investigating another case I'm working on. Silvia is a counselor at the high school."

"I know Ms. Cromwell. She was my counselor as well. Did she have an opinion as to what happened to Zane?"

"Not specifically, but during the course of our discussion, she mentioned the missing boys. She said that she first noticed a strong personality change in Kalen West. She specifically said that he began using terms such as personal power and one life about the same time he began cutting classes and acting out at home. I'm not sure if you know Kalen, but his parents recently split up, and he's been taking it hard. Ms. Cromwell suspected that it was his parent's divorce that led to his deviant behavior."

"I don't know Kalen well since he's much younger than me, but he was friends with Zane, so I know who he is." She sat forward. "So maybe all three boys met someone who put them on the path to personal power. Maybe their relationship with this person led to their disappearance." She paused. "Do you think Zane got mixed up in some sort of a cult?"

"Maybe. It does seem that the link between the three missing boys is their new commitment to personal power and making sure the one life they have to live is the one life they choose to live."

"So how do we figure out who this 'one life' guru is? How do we find Zane?"

I sat back in my chair. "I'm not sure yet. Give me a day to think things over. Can you meet tomorrow?"

"I can. Just tell me when and where."

"How about here. In the afternoon. Say around three o'clock?"

"I'll be here."

Chapter 10

Juggling two cases was going to be somewhat tricky, but I was all but totally convinced that once I spoke to Caroline Grant, I'd be able to close that case with a checkmark in the win column. Valerie had told me that she'd give Caroline my number and ask her to call me. I just hoped she would.

In the meantime, I was supposed to meet Cora at three o'clock this afternoon, and I really wanted to have something to tell her. I wasn't sure where to start, but physical activity usually helped me to think, so I got up early and set off for a run with the dogs. As winter faded and the long hot months of summer appeared on the horizon, I realized that the dogs and I would be spared the heat we'd had to suffer through living in the south. I was really looking forward to a summer of mild temperatures where running wouldn't become an activity best done late at night or inside an air-conditioned gym.

After the dogs and I finished our run, I took a shower and got dressed. As I sat on my deck looking out at the bay and sipping coffee, I considered where to start my investigation for the day. As I was speaking to Cora yesterday, it occurred to me that if the three boys had been introduced to someone who was filling their heads with concepts relating to personal power and one life, maybe someone had seen them together. Jemma seemed to be pretty tight with Zane's friend, Artie Drysdale. Perhaps another conversation with him was in order. Of course, today was Friday, and school had yet to let out for the summer, so it was unlikely I'd be able to speak to him before I met with Cora at three o'clock. Jemma might be able to get phone records for all three boys, so perhaps she was the best person to start with.

Taking my coffee mug into the kitchen and setting it in the sink, I grabbed my notepad and then headed next door to see if Jemma had a few minutes to chat.

"Ainsley," Jemma greeted. "Come on in."

"Thanks. I hate to interrupt you during the workday, but I wanted to talk to you briefly before I head out for the day."

"It's not a problem. I have work to get done, but nothing urgent. Coffee? I wouldn't mind taking a short break."

"Coffee would be great." I'd just had a cup, but when it came to coffee, a cup was rarely enough.

"So, what's on your mind?" Jemma asked after she'd poured us each a mug of coffee, and we'd settled on the deck."

"I had a visit from Cora Maddox yesterday."

She lifted a brow. "You don't say. What did Cora want?"

I filled her in on our conversation and shared with her the fact that I wasn't sure I was going to officially take the case but that I did plan to poke around today and see if I could pick up a lead. "I wanted to ask about the phone records for all three boys. Cora made the same comment others have made about all three missing boys having family issues. She also shared that Zane had made comments to her about personal power and one life, which seem to be terms that keep circling around."

"So you want to see if you can find a link between these phrases, the behavior issues, and the disappearance of all three boys."

"I do. The fact that all three used the same phrases can't be a coincidence. At this point, I figure that if we can trace the phrases back to the source, whether it be a book, a club, a guru, or a cult, we might be able to figure out what exactly is going on. I know that phone records won't link to the phrases, but if we can find a phone number associated with all three missing boys, that might give us a place to start."

"It does sound like a good place to jump in. I assume Deputy Todd has already pulled the cell records for all three boys, but it's unlikely he'll share. I'll work on it and see what I can do."

"Thank you. I appreciate that. I also thought I'd try talking to Artie Drysdale. You mentioned that he was good friends with Zane."

"He is. He doesn't know you, so I should probably go along. Maybe we can track him down after school."

"I'm supposed to meet Cora at three o'clock, and school doesn't let out until then, so it might have to wait for the weekend."

"It's Friday. The high school lets out at noon on Fridays. I'll text Artie and see if he has time to meet with us."

"Are you sure? I don't want to pull you away from work."

She shrugged. "I usually knock off early on Fridays anyway, and I'm actually pretty caught up. I'll just finish what I'm doing and then go to work on the phone numbers. Why don't you come back in about an hour."

"Okay, I will. And thank you."

"No need to thank me. I want to find those boys as much as anyone."

After I went back to my cottage, I decided to pull the high school yearbook up on my computer. I'd heard that the yearbook for this year had already been released, although I wasn't sure if it would be available online yet. I hoped it was. Maybe I could find a photo that might give me a hint as to what might have been going on in the lives of our missing teens.

After locating the yearbook, the first thing I did was look up each teen on the page that featured his individual photo. Zane was a good-looking kid with an athletic build. He had a nice smile that didn't quite reach his eyes but based on the image portrayed, I was willing to bet he was popular with the girls. The online edition of the yearbook contained links you could click on that took you to other photos and mentions of a student in the yearbook. Zane had a lot of links associated with his photo. Most of the links led to photos of the various athletic teams he participated in, but there were also casual photos of him at a school dance, a Friday night bonfire, and a fundraising dinner for the booster club.

Kalen was a tall kid with a mop of dark hair and a long scar on his cheek. He only had a few links to click on, which included a link to the page featuring the wrestling team and a link to a group photo taken at the high school auto shop.

Trevor was short and skinny. He had blond hair, a thin face, and serious-looking glasses. Trevor's "home page" had more links than Kalen's but less than Zane's. I clicked all the links to find that Trevor had memberships in a variety of academic clubs and organizations. I remembered that he was super smart, so I supposed that wasn't surprising.

By the time I'd finished looking through the yearbook, it was time to meet up with Jemma, so I turned my computer off and headed in that direction.

"Perfect timing," she said. "I got my project for work completed, and I managed to pull cell phone records for all three boys."

"And? Did you find any phone numbers the three had in common?"

"Just one. Underground Comics. Underground Comics is a comic book and video game store over on Edmonton Street. It's popular with a lot of high school-aged kids as well as quite a few adults, so it's not surprising that all three boys might have spent time there. Still, it is a lead, so I figured we could stop by after we speak to Artie."

"So you were able to get ahold of Artie?" I asked.

She nodded. "Artie has a full day planned today, but he said that if we want to ask him some questions, we should meet him at the school at noon right when he gets out. He said he'd wait for us on the bleachers located at the football field."

I glanced at my watch. It was already after eleven. "I guess we should head there first. If Artie doesn't know anything and the comic book and video game store turns out to be a dead-end, I guess we can take a second look at the phone logs this afternoon."

By the time Jemma freshened up a bit and grabbed her bag, it was time to head to the high school. Jemma volunteered to drive since she knew where everything was. I really appreciated the way Jemma was always willing to drop everything and help me. I'd offer to buy her lunch if she had time, but I supposed I'd have to wait and see how the afternoon went. I needed to be at the office by three o'clock, but that should still leave us time to eat unless Artie had news that provided an additional clue.

As he said he would be, Artie was waiting for us on the bleachers when Jemma and I arrived.

"Thanks for taking the time to meet with us," Jemma said to the tall boy with broad shoulders and sandy blond hair.

"If I can help you find Zane, I'm happy to do whatever is needed."

"When we spoke before, Zane's paddleboard had been found, but word about the other missing boys wasn't known yet. Now that you know that Zane, Kalen, and Trevor all turned up missing over the same three-day period, have you thought of anything else that might help us figure out what might be going on?" Jemma asked.

Artie swiveled his mouth to the right. He narrowed his gaze and then spoke. "There is something. I'm not sure if it's important, but after Kalen went missing, it occurred to me that I'd seen Zane and Kalen together a couple weeks ago."

"At school?" Jemma asked.

He shook his head. "No, in town. They were standing in front of Underground Comics talking. I was in the car with my mom. We were on our way home from a dentist appointment, so I didn't talk to them, but I did think it was sort of odd. Zane and Kalen used to be friends back when Kalen was still on the football team, but then Kalen decided to quit sports and focus on cars. I was sort of surprised when Kalen announced he wasn't going to do football this year, but since his dad is really into cars, I guess I sort of get it."

"Is Kalen's dad is a mechanic?" I asked.

"No. Not by profession, but Kalen's dad likes to restore old classics, and working in the garage on his latest project was something Kalen and his dad enjoyed doing together. After his dad left, Kalen started hanging out with the kids who hang out at the high school auto shop, and he stopped hanging out with the guys from the football team."

"So Kalen has always been interested in cars, but he really only tinkered with his father until his father left, and then he quit his other after-school activities and started hanging out with the car guys full time?"

Artie nodded. "Zane was pretty mad when Kalen quit football. The two worked well together, and Kalen leaving really hurt the team. After Kalen quit, Zane started avoiding him, which is why I was surprised to see the two of them hanging out together in front of the comic book and video game store."

"Did you ever ask Zane about it?" I asked.

"Sure. Zane said he was at the store to check out the new stock and just happened to run into Kalen. I guess it could have happened that way. I didn't think a whole lot about it until both friends went missing."

"What about Trevor?" I asked. "Have you ever seen him at the comic book and video game store?"

"Sure, all the time. Trevor is a geeky kid, and like a lot of geeky kids, he's totally into fantasy and role-playing."

"Role-playing?" I asked.

"There are a few games out there. Dungeons and Dragons is a board game that has been around for a long time. Everyone who is into role-playing has played, but there are other board games as well. In addition to the role-playing board games, there are multiplayer video games that are even more popular at the moment."

"Was Zane involved in any of these games?" I asked.

"Sure. We both are. Kalen and Trevor too. Role-playing games are huge, but I guess you know that."

"Can you think of a game that utilizes catchphrases such as personal power and one life?" I asked.

He frowned. "Not specifically, although personal power makes me think of being strong and fearless, which is the key to winning most of the games."

Artie took a few minutes to describe the setup of a few of the games he and Zane had been involved in recently. None of them sounded like the sort of thing that might cause a major shift in behavior, but they all allowed the player to step out of their lives and be someone else. Someone, I realized, in control of their destiny in a way that an average fifteen-year-old boy might not be. Especially a fifteen-year-old boy with life issues being played out within the family dynamic.

"Had Zane been spending more time playing video games lately than he previously did?" Jemma asked.

Artie nodded. "He's canceled plans with me in favor of just staying home and playing games, so I suspect he got hooked on something. I like playing, but video games aren't the most important thing to me. I'd rather go out and hang with friends. Zane used to be more like me, but I will admit that lately, he seemed to really be into the whole online thing."

Artie had plans to meet up with friends, so Jemma and I thanked him and then headed toward the comic book and video game store. When we arrived, the place was packed, but school had just let out, so we decided to go and have lunch and then come back in the hope that some of the after-school crowd would have cleared out by then.

"You know, the more I think about it, the more convinced I am that a role-playing game might be the key we're looking for," Jemma said as we nibbled on seafood salads and freshly baked bread. "I've participated in a number of online games and have to admit that they can be very addicting. Not only is it hard to stop once you start, but the more invested you become in your character, the stronger the reality of that character becomes in your mind."

"So, do you think that Zane, Kalen, and Trevor might have been playing the same game?" I asked.

"I think it's possible. Since you play the game as a character and not as yourself, it opens the door for participants to engage in dialogue as well as quests with people they might not hang out with in another situation. Zane is a popular jock and Trevor is a nerdy science geek, so they don't really hang out at school, but if Zane's character and Trevor's character are allies during the game, then it's totally possible that the two boys might feel a bond of sorts even if it is a bond that exists primarily within the game."

"Okay," I said. "I think the online multiplayer game idea is one worth checking out. I can see how a game that somehow fulfills the needs of a fifteen-year-old boy having a hard time at home or at school might become addicting to the point of providing a brainwashing effect of sorts."

"Exactly. It sounds like all three boys found themselves in situations where they are suffering from a lack of control in their own lives. Zane's sister, who had been a buffer of sorts between Zane and their father, went off to college, leaving Zane to deal with the rigid and controlling man on his own. It sounds like Kalen was closer to his father than he was to his mother, and it created a void in his life when his father left. And Trevor seems to be struggling with the challenge of balancing his intellect with new social needs that might be rising to the surface as he matures. I can see where a game which allows all three boys to be in total control of their lives might prove to be addicting."

"Of course, even if we can prove this theory, and even if we can find the specific game where the term one life is utilized, we'll still need to figure out how the game led to the disappearance of three of the players and where they might be now."

Jemma and I agreed that our theory, even if it turned out to be correct, was only a start if we actually wanted to find the boys, which we did; but a start was the first step in any successful investigation, so we finished our lunch and headed toward the comic book and video game store.

"Can I help you?" a tall skinny man who looked to be in his late twenties to early thirties asked after Jemma and I entered Underground Comics through the front door.

"My name is Ainsley Holloway." I offered the man a business card. "I'm a private investigator who's been hired to find out what happened to Zane Maddox. I wondered if you might be willing to answer a few questions."

He shrugged. "I don't know nothing about those missing kids, but if you want to ask me some questions, go ahead. I'll answer those I can."

"Zane Maddox, Kalen West, and Trevor Wilson are all currently missing. I understand that all three frequented this store."

"Yeah. So, what? Half the kids who attend the high school, including a fair number of girls, come here. What does frequenting my store have to do with anything?"

"I'm not saying that frequenting your store is in any way connected to whatever happened to the boys," I said. "I just hoped that since all three missing kids came in here, you might know a bit about them. We're talking to everyone who knew any of the boys."

The man seemed to relax a bit. I supposed it was natural for one to feel defensive when being interviewed about missing persons.

"I guess I did know all three missing boys. What do you want to know?"

I leaned an elbow on the counter and turned my body just a bit so I could look at the man directly. "I understand that Zane, Kalen, and Trevor all enjoyed playing multiplayer games online."

"Sure. Most of the kids who hang out here are into the role-playing stuff to a degree."

"I assume that some of the kids who come in here take the game a lot more seriously than others."

"Yeah. I guess that's true. A lot of players jump in the game when they have some free time, but a few of my more dedicated customers seem to make a lifestyle of it."

"And the three boys who are missing? Which type were they?" I asked.

He stroked his shaggy beard before answering. "Zane stopped in most days, and I know he was online most nights and often on weekends. Actually, he's been online a lot more regularly lately. I think the End Days mission he got involved in really drew him in."

"And the others?"

He scratched a cheek. "Kalen didn't come into the store as often as Zane, who stopped in almost every day, at least for a few months, but he has been online more often since joining the same End Days mission that Zane is involved in. Trevor too, for that matter."

"And the game?" I asked. "What exactly is the objective?"

He shrugged. "It's really all about surviving in the world that you've been forced into. Sort of a post-apocalypse thing."

"And Zane, Kalen, and Trevor all have roles in this game?" I verified.

"Yep. And all three were doing really well and climbing up in the ranking until they went missing."

"And have they played since they went missing?" I asked.

He frowned. "I'm not sure. I guess if knowing that is important, I can take a look at the activity logs for each of the boys."

"You can track their play?" Jemma asked.

"For this specific game, I can. The creator provided a program that all those who play can sign up for. Once you're signed up for the program and playing the game, stats are made available to both the user and everyone else with an account. The program allows all the players to track play and ranking for themselves and their competitors. Most gamers are competitive, and they want to see their name, or at least their username, up on the leader board, so they sign up and allow access to their user logs."

"And how exactly does one get listed on the leader board?" I asked.

"You can make it to the board by logging a lot of hours or leveling up."

"Leveling up?" I asked.

"Winning one level and making it to the next."

"And how do you win End Days?" Jemma asked. "What is the overall objective?"

"The objective is ascendance, and the way to be invited to ascend is to make it to the final level. I'm not sure what level that might be since no one I know has ever achieved it, but supposedly once you reach the final level, you leave the challenging world you've been fighting to survive in behind and enter some sort of nirvana. I heard that there are only a few who have gotten that far in the game. Like I said, I've never spoken to anyone who has actually ascended, but I heard there was a team in New Mexico who managed to ascend around the first of March and another team in California who conquered the game just a month or so after that. I guess you can ask them about it if you can track down anyone from those two teams, but as far as I know, they aren't sharing their experience, so the whole thing is really mysterious."

"You were going to check the activity log to tell me when the three missing boys from Gooseberry Bay played last," I reminded him.

"Oh, sure." He pulled up a log on his computer. "The log only shows usernames, which might not help others, but since the boys are in here so often and we chat, I know the usernames of all three."

"And what are their usernames?" I asked.

"Zane is Trident, Kalen is Raith, and Trevor is Hadron." He typed in a few commands, pulling up the sheet he was looking for. "It looks as if all three boys logged a serious number of hours Friday afternoon into early Saturday morning, but none have played since."

"Did anything odd happen in the game Friday or Saturday?" Jemma asked. "Something unique or significant that might explain why the three boys played so long Friday afternoon into early Saturday morning but then quit playing altogether."

"I wasn't online, and I haven't managed to reach the level the three of them have, so I really have no idea what might have happened in the game. I suppose the boys may have quit playing because they went missing."

"Kalen was last seen Saturday, but Zane didn't turn up missing until late in the day Sunday, and Trevor was actually home all weekend and didn't turn up missing until Monday afternoon, yet none of the boys logged into the game after they logged out early Saturday morning."

The man crossed his arms over his chest. "I really have no idea why they didn't log in over the weekend. Like I said, only one other local team has made it past level fifteen, and no team made it as far as these three have, so I doubt you'll find anyone who will know what sort of challenges they faced and why they might have decided to quit when they did."

"Can you provide the names of anyone who was logged into the game Friday afternoon and early Saturday morning at the same time as Zane and the others were?" I asked. "I realize they might not be on the same level, but they might have interacted. Shared tips. That sort of thing."

"There are a lot of players if you take into account all the levels. Only one other local team has made it past level fifteen. I would guess if there was chatter, it would be between Zane's group and the guys who had leveled up to level twenty and the other local group currently on level eighteen."

"And who was in this group on level eighteen?" I asked.

"Zork, Halo, and Nomad. It appears the three have formed an aligned team."

"Aligned?" I asked.

"Once you reach level fifteen, the only way to continue successfully is to form an alliance. Zane, Kalen, and Trevor formed an alliance when they all reached level fifteen around the same time. Since then, when they play, they play together."

"And do you know the real names of Zork, Halo, and Nomad?" I asked.

"Actually, I don't. I guess I can ask around if you think it's important."

"I'd appreciate that," I said as I turned to leave. Just as we reached the door, Jemma turned back. "Do the words *one life* mean anything to you? Is that phrase part of the game?"

"Sure. As I just indicated, once you pass level fourteen and enter level fifteen, you form alliances for the quest ahead, which is the only way to make it to the final level where you're invited to ascend. The mantra most recited by those who enter this quest is: 'One life to live, one life to give.'"

Chapter 11

I had to admit I was nervous about meeting with Cora. The mantra: "One life to live one life to give" conjured all sorts of unpleasant images in my mind. As she indicated she would, Cora showed up at my office at exactly three o'clock.

"So?" she asked. "Do you have news?"

I hesitated. "Perhaps. I'm honestly not sure that the information I've been able to dig up is relevant, but it seems that Zane enjoyed playing video games."

"So? All teenage boys enjoy playing video games."

"I guess that's mostly true, but I found out that Zane was involved in a multiplayer online role-playing game called End Days. As it turns out, Kalen and Trevor were players in the same online game."

She just looked at me as if waiting for me to get to the point.

"I spoke to the man who was working the counter at the comic book and video game store today. He told me that Zane, Kalen, and Trevor had all been logging a lot of hours and that they'd all achieved a really high ranking and ultimately formed an alliance with one another for the quest ahead. I have to admit I don't know a lot about online gaming, but it seems that all three were really into it and put a lot of hours into climbing through the levels."

"That sounds like Zane. He's always liked video games, and he does tend to become obsessive when things are rough at home. The rougher things are with Dad, the more hours he spends in his make-believe world, working hard to collect make-believe stuff. I guess I get it. It's a good escape. But what does that have to do with the fact that he went missing?"

"Apparently, the goal of the game has to do with passing through levels, each with their own unique challenge until you reach the final level where you are invited to ascend."

"Ascend?"

"I'm not sure what that means exactly. The guy from the video game store made it sound like the majority of the game is spent in some sort of post-apocalyptic world, and once you make it through all the levels, you ascend to some sort of perfect place. He referred to it as a type of nirvana."

"Okay. So?"

"I guess those who make it to level fifteen are teamed up and sent on a quest of some sort. Apparently, the mantra recited by those who have entered the final quest is: 'One life to live, one life to give.'"

Her eyes grew wide. "One life."

I nodded. "Exactly. I can't know for certain that the game had anything to do with Zane going missing, but the man I spoke to was somehow able to look at user logs, and he told me that Zane, Kalen, and Trevor logged some serious hours Friday afternoon into early Saturday morning, but that none of them has logged in since."

"So what does this mean? How does this help us find them?"

"I'm not sure," I admitted. "It did occur to me that perhaps Zane left clues for someone to find. Have you had a chance to look around in his room since you've been back?"

"No. It never occurred to me to do so. Zane would have a fit if he knew."

"Under the circumstances, I think that a peek at his personal space is a good idea. Do you know if Deputy Todd has been by to take a look?"

She slowly moved her head from right to left and then back again. "I don't know. I spoke to Deputy Todd a bunch of times, but I haven't seen him since I've been home. Do you think we should look now?"

I hesitated. "Do you think your parents will mind?"

She shook her head. "Dad is working and said he'd be late tonight, and Mom went to my aunt's house since she didn't want to be home alone. I don't expect either of them until after dinner. If you want to come with me now, we can be in and out before either of them get back."

"Okay," I said. "Let's go and take a look. I'm not sure we'll find anything, but at this point, we need any sort of clue we can manage to dig up."

As I expected it would be, the Maddox home was a large home on a large lot with a view of the water. As Cora had indicated, no one was home when we arrived, so she invited me in, and we headed directly to Zane's room. I half expected to find a mess since the few teenage males I'd known growing up tended to have messy rooms, but Zane's room was actually pretty neat. The bed was made, the desk arranged neatly, and the television and video game system was tucked neatly into shelving built into the wall.

"So what are we looking for?" Cora asked.

"I'm not really sure. If Zane was a girl, I'd say to look for a diary or journal. I don't suppose Zane kept anything like that."

"Not that I know of. If he did, it would be on his computer rather than in a book."

I glanced at the desk, which held a laptop, printer, and external drive I assumed was for backup. "I don't suppose you can get into Zane's laptop?"

She shrugged. "Zane probably has it password protected, but we can take a look." She opened the unit and turned the power on. As predicted, the first screen to pop up asked for a six-letter passcode.

"Any ideas?" I asked.

She tried five or six different things, but none worked. She paused to think things over as I continued to look around. Deciding to turn on the video game system, I hit the power button. Unlike the computer, which featured a gate with a code before one could proceed, the video game console went directly to the home page when the power was turned on.

I paused to look more closely at the home page. There were icons for a bunch of games and a folder that contained links to games I suspected were older and no longer used much. There were links to various online groups, along with a folder with notes and what appeared to be usernames and codes of some sort.

I noticed a headset on a nearby table. I supposed that was how the gamer communicated with his or her team as well as their opponents.

"Do you play?" I asked Cora.

"No. You?"

"Not really." I picked up the controller and began to poke around a bit. "I think these games have message boards and chat rooms so the gamers can communicate with each other. The thing is, I'm not sure how to find what I'm looking for."

Cora just stood staring at me.

"I'm going to call my friend, Jemma. She'll know. She can probably even walk me through it on the phone."

As it turned out, Jemma knew exactly what to do. She told me what to click on and what to look for. When I got to the message center, I noticed that Zane had used the message feature to send and receive messages. I was really only interested in messages sent or received Friday, Saturday, and Sunday before Zane leaving the house, never to be seen again.

"There's a message Friday morning to Zane from someone with the username Hadron, who I know is actually Trevor. They seemed to be making arrangements to go on a quest. There is also a message from someone with the username Raith, who I know is Kalen, confirming a meet-up Saturday evening." I looked up at Cora. "I don't suppose you know what Zane did Saturday?"

She shook her head. "I have no idea. It's been a couple weeks since we spoke."

I continued to look through the log. "There are three messages Sunday that seem to relate to a meeting of some sort between Trident, who the guy at the comic book and video game store told me is really Zane, and three individuals: Raith, Hadron, and Reaper." I looked at Cora. "I know that Raith is Kalen and Hadron is Trevor, but I have no idea who Reaper is. I wonder if it would be okay to take the video game console so my friend, Jemma, can have a look at it. She's a computer genius, and if there are clues on this unit, she'd be much more likely to find them than I am."

"Yeah. Okay. I'm sure no one will miss it. Just tell your friend to be careful not to mess up any of Zane's stuff. When he gets home, he's going to be pissed if he finds we erased his high scores or all the imaginary stuff he's collected."

"I'll tell her to be careful." I began unplugging the unit. I glanced at the desk. "Maybe I should take the computer as well."

She looked less sure but eventually agreed. I promised to call her tomorrow and let her know what, if anything, we'd found. If we did find something that seemed like a clue, maybe we could convince Kalen's mom and Trevor's parents to let us look at their video game consoles as well.

I'd just pulled into the parking area for the cottages when my phone rang. Once I'd started forwarding my calls from Ainsley Holloway Investigations to my cell when I wasn't in my office, I'd begun answering my phone whether or not I'd recognized the caller ID.

"This is Ainsley Holloway," I answered.

"Hi, Ainsley. My name is Caroline Brolin. I used to be Caroline Grant before I married. I spoke to Valerie, and she briefly filled me in on your quest to find the owner of a charm bracelet from the nineties. She suggested I call you."

My heart rate increased just a bit. Caroline had to be the one I was looking for. She checked almost all the boxes. I just hoped she'd be willing to tell her story so I could confirm what I was sure I already knew.

"I'm afraid I'm not the person you're looking for, nor do I know who is," she continued.

Talk about having the wind knocked out of your sails. I was so sure that Caroline would be the owner of the bracelet.

"Yes, it is true that I participated in the Bay to Boardwalk Run in nineteen ninety-six, and I also completed the Brewster's Books Reading Challenge," she continued. "I did date a man who showed up on a yacht, and I did volunteer at both the carnival and on movie nights. Based on the charms displayed, that particular bracelet really could have belonged to me, but it didn't. I'm so sorry. You must really want to find this woman to go to so much trouble."

"I really appreciate you calling me and letting me know," I said. "I will admit that I felt fairly certain that you were the one."

"I understand. Like I said, given the clues you have to work with, it really could have been mine."

"Are you sure you don't have any idea who the bracelet might have belonged to? It's possible you might have run into the person who did own the bracelet since you ran in the run, participated in the reading challenge, and volunteered for the carnival and movie nights."

She paused before she answered. "I have to admit I was pretty absorbed with Justin that summer, so I wasn't paying a lot of attention to anyone else. Valerie said you had a list of names. If you want to read them to me, maybe I'll recognize someone."

I took my sheet of paper with the seven names out. "So far, I've spoken to everyone from the original list with the exception of Rosalie Watts and Naomi Potter."

"I'm sorry, but neither name rings a bell. If you'd like, I can think on it a bit, and if I come up with a name, I can call you back."

"I'd appreciate that. Thank you for offering."

After I hung up, I took the lists we'd come up with out again. It looked like I was running out of names. Perhaps we'd missed something, and the owner of the bracelet was someone other than one of the seven people who'd participated in both the run and the reading challenge. It was possible Naomi was the person we were looking for. One of the charms was an ice cream cone, and someone named Naomi had worked at an ice cream shop that summer. I planned to talk to Troy Trauner tomorrow after the kiddie carnival. Maybe he'd be able to shine a light on things. Ellery was leaving town Sunday. I supposed I could continue to dig around after she left, but I really wanted to put this mystery to bed before she drove onto the ferry.

I'd just hung up with Caroline when Parker pulled into the lot. She informed me that she was there to see Jemma and ask a favor of her, so I explained about the computer and video game console, and she suggested we head over to the roommates' cottage together. I agreed that might be a good idea, but I wanted to let Kai and Kalie out for a bathroom break before bringing them over, so Parker agreed to take possession of the computer and video game console and deliver them to Jemma while I took care of the dogs.

Jemma logged on and was able to navigate the video game console. She confirmed that the messages we'd found weren't the only messages associated with the account and was able to pull up the activity log that I hadn't been able to find.

Jemma began to speak. "Based on the message history, it looks as if Zane, who as we already know, went by the username Trident, began sending messages to and receiving messages from Raith, Hadron, and Reaper, as well as a handful of others a few months ago."

"The guy from the video game store mentioned that Halo, Zork, and Nomad were another team currently participating in the quest," I reminded her. "He said that he wasn't sure who any of them really were."

"The message sent Sunday relating to a meeting involved Raith, Hadron, Trident, and Reaper," Jemma informed us.

"If we're right about the usernames, and Kalen actually is Raith, then at least we know that Kalen was alive and well Sunday even though he hadn't been seen since Saturday," Parker pointed out.

"That's a good point," I said. I thought about the man at the comic book and video game store. "When we spoke to the man in the comic book and video game store, I felt like he might know more than he admitted. Perhaps we should talk to him again. If nothing else, it would really be helpful to know who this Reaper is."

"I'll go and talk to him," Parker offered. "The two of you stay here and work on getting any useful information you can out of that video game console as well as that computer." Parker grabbed her purse. "I'll bring dinner back with me. Will Josie be here?"

"Yes," Jemma answered. "She'll be home in about an hour."

"Is Chinese food okay?" Parker asked.

"Chinese sounds good," Jemma commented. She glanced at the computer on the table. "I don't suppose you know either Kalen's mother or one of Trevor's parents."

"Not well," Parker asked. "Why do you ask?"

"If we had the video game consoles of the other two missing teens, it would give us a lot more information than having just one will."

"I'll get them," Parker said. "I'll go and talk to the guy at the comic book and video game store, and then I'll see if I can get the other two video game consoles. I'll pick up dinner and then be back. I guess it might be a couple hours, so go ahead and have a snack if you're hungry."

After Parker left, Jemma continued to work, and I put a cheese and fruit tray together. I figured Josie would be hungry when she got home, so it seemed like a good idea to have something ready.

"It looks like Zane first entered the game four months ago," Jemma informed me. "It took about two and a half months to get past the first fourteen levels. Once he managed to do that, he joined Hadron and Raith, forming an alliance of sorts. While it looks as if Zane played the game fairly often while working on the first fourteen levels, I don't notice a real push until after he teamed up with the others."

"Do we know if Hadron and Raith started at the same time?" I asked.

Jemma shook her head. "I don't know when they started playing the game or how many hours they spent on the game until they joined forces with Zane. Zane's video game console only shows me his playing history. It appears that the quest is more of a solo pursuit until level fifteen is reached."

"So the three have only been working together for a little over a month." I stated.

"About five and a half weeks based on what I can figure out from Zane's gaming history." She navigated through a few pages of the log. "It looks like they've been logging some serious hours. If their grades are falling or other interests have been ignored, I can see why."

"Does it appear that anyone else is on the team? Is it always just the three of them?"

"It looks like it's just the three of them on the same team, although there are messages between Zane and members of other teams."

Josie showed up a short time later. She ran upstairs to change out of her work clothes while I set the fruit and cheese tray out on the counter. Jemma was still surfing around in the video game console's memory, but she had made the comment that she wasn't coming up with a lot, so perhaps she'd turn her attention to the computer.

"You'll never believe who came into the restaurant today," Josie said once she had changed clothes and joined us downstairs.

"Who?" Jemma asked as she tried to figure out a way into Zane's computer.

"Prentice Caldwell." Josie looked at me. "Prentice Caldwell used to live in Gooseberry Bay, but she left town after creating a huge scandal a couple years ago."

"Huge scandal?" I asked.

"She was using her skills with the computer to hack into the email accounts of some of the local big wigs in order to find dirt that she could then use to blackmail them."

"Shouldn't she be in jail?" I asked.

"She should be," Josie agreed. "The thing is that while what she was doing seemed obvious, the men she blackmailed refused to admit to the blackmail or testify in court. I guess they didn't want to have their dirty laundry aired during the trial, so they all made statements about the money they'd been paying her being compensation for services rendered. Everyone knew what was really going on. Everyone knew that these men had decided to cover for her in order to save their own skin, but the DA didn't have a case if the victims of the blackmail wouldn't agree to file a complaint, so when Prentice decided to move away, the district attorney decided to drop it."

"So why'd she come back?" I asked.

"She said she came back to talk to some people who she felt might be able to help figure out what had happened to Kalen."

"She knows Kalen?" Jemma asked.

"I guess that Kalen's father was one of her blackmail victims with whom she eventually entered into a physical relationship. According to Prentice, she continued to stay in contact with Kalen's father after she left, and once Kalen's parents split up, they even moved in together."

I remembered hearing that Kalen's father had had an affair. I guess Prentice was the one he'd had it with. "It seems odd to me that this man would enter into a romantic relationship with the woman who'd been blackmailing him," I said.

"I totally agree," Josie responded. "But that's what happened, and when Kalen went missing, Prentice decided to see if she could find something out from one of her contacts."

"And did she find something out?" Jemma asked.

"Actually, she did. Prentice told me that one of the men she knew from when she'd lived here before had seen Zane, Kalen, and Trevor together Sunday evening."

"Where?" Jemma asked.

"Down at the marina. It was late. The marina staff had gone home, and the boat rental place was closed. This person told Prentice that the boys were sitting on the dock at the very south end of the harbor, talking. He'd come in late on his boat, so he didn't talk to them. He just tied up and left. But he's sure it was them since the dock has all those overhead lights, and he had to ferry his way right past them to make his way to his assigned slip."

"Okay, so if that's true, then all three boys were still alive and together after Kalen had been missing a full day and Zane had left home with his paddleboard," I said. "I wonder what they were doing."

Josie shrugged. "I don't know. Prentice didn't know, and neither did her contact. He just told her that he'd seen the three boys, but that was the extent of it."

"Hopefully, Parker will know more by the time she gets back," Jemma said.

"Where is Parker?" Josie asked.

"She went to look into a few things and to grab dinner for us. She should be here in an hour or so."

"I'm starving," Josie said. "I think I'll grab a snack."

"I made a cheese and fruit tray," I shared.

"I was thinking something more filling. Maybe a few crackers to go with the cheese."

I joined Josie in the kitchen while Jemma continued to work on the laptop. Once Parker arrived with the food, we focused on the meal. It was after we'd eaten when I asked Parker what she'd been able to find out.

"I was able to confirm that Kalen is definitely Raith and Trevor is definitely Hadron. I can also confirm that Zane is Trident and that all the boys had been logging a serious amount of hours before their disappearance. I also confirmed that the three boys had only been working together for the past five or six weeks."

"And no one you spoke to knew what sort of tasks the boys were facing in the game once they began their final quest?" I asked.

"No, no one I spoke to knew that," Parker confirmed.

"I'll poke around and see what I can find," Jemma offered. "Maybe I can strike up a conversation with one of the other players who have surpassed level fourteen. I do have Zane's video game console. It wouldn't be all that hard to slip my way in. The trick will be to find something out before anyone realizes that I'm not actually Zane."

"I'll ask around," Josie said. "Maybe we can figure out who Reaper, Zork, Halo, and Nomad are. If they were signed up for the ranking system, then chances are they're local."

Parker jumped in. "Oh, I meant to tell you that I spoke to Kalen's mother, and she's going to bring his video game console by the Rambling Rose tomorrow." She looked at Josie. "You mentioned that you'd be working, so I figured that was easiest."

"I'll watch for her," she said.

"I haven't gotten ahold of either of Trevor's parents yet," Parker added. "I'll keep trying. Other than that, we just keep doing what we do. We talk to people, and we look for clues."

"I'm volunteering at the kiddie carnival tomorrow," I said.

"Me too," Jemma joined in.

"And Josie and I are working," Parker said. "How about we all meet up here again tomorrow evening."

Everyone confirmed that would work and we agreed to meet at five o'clock. Perhaps we'd get a break between now and then. The idea that the boys were out there, waiting to be rescued was one I couldn't get out of my head, although given the fact that the boys were all seen together on Sunday after Zane left home also had me considering the fact that the three boys had simply taken off for some reason and were actually okay.

Chapter 12

Jemma and I decided to ride to the kiddie carnival in the park together the following day. The event was set to open at nine and run until two. There were carnival-type games such as a ring toss, a dart game, and a basketball toss, plus there were food vendors selling a variety of items that could be enjoyed on one of the long tables that had been set up. The event was a fundraiser for the elementary school, so it was mostly kids in the five to twelve age range that swarmed the area.

"Oh, good, you're both here on time," Hope said when Jemma and I approached the table that had been set up for the volunteers.

"We're here and ready to work," Jemma confirmed. "Where do you want me?"

"The ring toss. You did it last year, so you know what to do." Hope then looked at me. "I thought I'd have you work the ticket booth with Darla. She can explain the pricing options."

"Okay." I looked around. "It looks like the tickets are being sold at that table near the park entrance."

Hope nodded. "If you have any questions, just ask Darla. The line is manageable right now, but it's going to get busy once the lunch hour approaches."

Hope was right. It did get busier as the morning wore on. Thankfully, ticket sales was an easy gig and didn't involve refereeing like some of the games, where determining whether someone won or not was often nothing more than a judgment call.

"So, is this your first year helping with this event?" Darla asked after I'd introduced myself to her.

"It is. I just moved to Gooseberry Bay in the fall."

"So how are you liking it?" she asked as she counted out twenty tickets for a woman with two young children.

"I love it. Everyone has been so nice, and the area is simply gorgeous."

Darla handed the woman her tickets and then began counting out tickets for the next customer. "Are you working locally?"

"Actually, I recently opened my own private investigation firm."

"Of course. I've seen that across the boardwalk. You're next to Then and Again. I love poking around in there." She handed the woman her tickets and then smiled at the next customer in line. "I imagine being a PI is interesting."

"It can be," I said as a second line began to form, and I had my own customer to count out tickets for. Things got busy at this point, so our conversation paused, but once the line had been taken care of, Darla jumped back in.

"So what sorts of things do you look into as a PI?" she asked.

I shrugged. "A variety of things. I'm currently working on helping a woman track down the owner of a charm bracelet." I took a few minutes to go over what we had and what we were looking for. I'd spoken to Ellery this morning, and she'd shared that she'd run into a bit of a dead-end as well. She'd been showing the bracelet around town, but while there were some who had theories relating to a specific charm, no one had been able to match a person with the bracelet. I'd told her when we spoke that I had plans to meet with the man at the ice cream shop once I finished at the event at the park, and she shared that she wanted to talk to few more vendors on the boardwalk this morning.

Darla and I chatted about my cases, at least the ones I felt I could share, and her job as a bookkeeper for the town. She knew all about the missing boys, and she shared her concern that they might have met with foul play. I didn't mention that I was looking into things, but I did ask questions about the parents of the missing kids, and some of her comments only served to cement the fact that there had been trouble in all three households before the teens disappearing.

Around noon, Darla was sent to work one of the booths, and I was left alone with the tickets. By this point, the majority of folks who planned to show up were already there, so foot traffic at the ticket booth was minimal. At one-thirty, Jemma came over after being relieved of game duty.

"How's it going?" I asked.

"Fine. I have to admit I'm beginning to get bored. It was more fun before Darla left."

"Only thirty more minutes, and then we're done. I'll sit with you until then."

"So you're done for the day?"

She nodded. "Things are slowing down. Most of the kids have used up their tickets and are eating or have even headed home. Did you ever get the chance to eat anything?"

"No. I figured I'd grab something after I was done."

"I haven't eaten either. Let's pop by the ice cream shop like we planned and then we can head over to one of the restaurants on Main Street and grab some lunch."

Jemma and I tracked Hope down once we were given the okay by one of the other organizers to shut down the ticket booth.

"Thank you both so much," she said.

"Happy to help," I responded. "It was fun to see all the kids come through. Do they have this type of event often?"

"Three or four times a year. There's the fundraiser in May, the event in the park on the Fourth of July, and, of course, the harvest festival. Sometimes, they do an indoor event at the elementary school just before the Christmas break. Personally, I think four is a bit much. It's a lot of work putting this all together."

"Maybe you should eliminate the July event since the traveling carnival comes through in July. It might not be here for the Fourth of July, but it does feature similar games."

"I might suggest that to the committee," Hope said. "We could still have the fireworks and the picnic but skip the games. Of course, the kids won't be happy about that. Maybe we could do another event that would engage them, but not be as much work."

The three of us continued to chat for a few minutes, and then Jemma and I said our goodbyes and headed for the ice cream shop. I'd been told that Tony Trauner would be on-site today. I just hoped he would be. The other employees I'd seen to date were much too young to have known or remember anyone who might have worked for the old shop back in the nineties.

"There was a Naomi who worked here back in the nineties, but her last name was Swenson," Tony informed us after we explained about the bracelet and the woman we were trying to track down.

"So you don't think she could be the woman who owned the bracelet we described?" I asked.

"No. I don't think so. Naomi Swenson was a local girl who worked summers for me all through high school. She never left the area and, in fact, still lives here, so I suppose you can speak to her, but I know for a fact that she was never pregnant as a teen or young woman. She married two years ago, but she still doesn't have any children."

Well, that was disappointing. We were running out of names, and I really wanted to get this wrapped up today.

"Does the name Rosalie Watts mean anything to you?" Jemma asked about the last name on our original list.

"Sure. Although, Rosalie went by Rose. I don't know anyone who referred to her by her given name."

I glanced at Jemma. She lifted a brow.

"So did Rose work here?" I asked Tony.

He nodded. "Rose only worked here for one summer, but I remember her. She was such a sweet thing, who just happened to be going through a tough time."

"Rosalie Watts completed the Bay to Boardwalk Run, and she completed the Brewster's Books Reading Challenge," I said to the man. "She might be the one we're looking for." I pulled up the photos on my phone. "One of the charms is even a rose. We thought that the rose represented a flower shop or garden, but it could simply have been included due to her name."

"Rose was seventeen that summer. She lived in Seattle but came to Gooseberry Bay for the season. I seem to remember that she came with a church group that brought teens to the area to work at the summer camp just outside of town."

"Summer camp?" I asked.

"It was a church camp serving underprivileged kids who were brought in for two-week stays. Teens from the city lived on-site and worked as counselors. Most of the teens who worked the camp also had part-time jobs in town, so they'd have spending money. The church group provided housing for the counselors, but not a wage, so Rose worked part-time for me."

"This could be her," Jemma said. "What can you tell us about her?"

"She was a quiet little thing. Shy. Sort of skittish. She worked at the camp in the mornings, but then she was free from mid-afternoon until the following morning. She worked about twenty hours a week for me. She didn't seem to have a lot of friends, but she did participate. She volunteered for the movie nights, and I think she helped out with some of the local fundraising events. I seem to remember that she worked the carnival when it was in town. She stayed busy."

"Did Rose have a boyfriend?" I asked.

He slowly shook his head. "Not that I remember. Like I said, she was the quiet sort. I do remember this one guy. I think he was just a friend and not a boyfriend, though. He was about her age. Maybe a year or two older. He came in a few times looking for Rose."

"Do you remember a name?" I asked.

He paused. It appeared he was thinking over my question. "I think his name was Noah. I'm pretty sure he'd graduated high school the previous spring. Now that I think about it, I'm pretty sure he was only in Gooseberry Bay for a short time before joining the Navy."

Rosalie, like Caroline, seemed to check all the boxes. The question was, if Rose didn't live in town and hadn't been seen since nineteen ninety-six, how on earth were we going to find her now?

"I don't suppose you have contact information for Rose," I wondered.

"I have an address in Seattle, but it's over twenty years old. I doubt Rose still lives with her parents. She's probably married by now, so I doubt she even has the same last name."

"At this point, Rosalie Watts is the only lead we have," I said, hoping that the man believed our story and didn't think us to be stalkers. "If you'd be willing to share the address you have on file, maybe we'll be able to use that as a starting point to track her down."

He hesitated.

"I know giving out employee information is probably frowned on, even if that information is a quarter of a century old, but if we can help my client find her mother…" I let the thought dangle.

"Are you sure the mother of this woman wants to be found? It seems to me that if the mother of this girl left her in a church and never once reached out after that point, she probably wants to stay anonymous."

"Then why leave the bracelet?" Jemma asked.

The man shrugged. "Okay. I'll give you what I have. I doubt it will be useful after all these years, but I guess if the mother of this woman, whether she actually is Rose or someone else, must have wanted to keep the door open for some future meeting, or she wouldn't have left a clue."

Once Tony had provided me the last known address he had for Rosalie, Jemma and I thanked him and left. We headed to lunch, and after ordering, I took a moment to call Ellery and let her know what we'd found. She was excited that we had a name, although I think even she realized that finding the woman with little more than a name and a twenty-five-year-old address would not be easy. I promised her that once we got back to the cottage, Jemma would get on the computer and see what she could find, and I also promised to call her with the results of our search no matter what we did or didn't find.

Chapter 13

As it turned out, Jemma was able to do quite a lot with the information we'd received that afternoon. Based on the address provided, Jemma was able to determine that Rosalie's parents were named Edward and Anna. Edward was the minister at a small church in Seattle, and Anna served the congregation by visiting the elderly and sick and helping to feed those in need. Edward and Anna Watts had five children. Four boys, two older than Rosalie, the only girl, and two younger. As Tony had indicated, the church ran a summer camp for underprivileged youth in Gooseberry Bay during the nineteen nineties. The counselors were mainly teens, aged sixteen to eighteen, who volunteered to help out. There were four paid staff members: the camp administrator, a woman named Lora Wilder, the cook, a woman named Elise Crenshaw, a male head counselor, a man named Elroy Winters, and a female head counselor, a woman named Polly Bolton.

There were group photos from each of the eight summers the group ran the camp. The photo for nineteen ninety-six featured, among others, a woman with dark hair and a shy smile, who really did look an awful lot like Ellery.

"I think we found your client's mother," Jemma said.

I gently nibbled on my lower lip, a habit I often retreated to when I felt nervous or uncertain. "Maybe." I looked at the photo closely. "The question in my mind is, why would this young woman abandon her baby in a church? Rosalie was part of an intact family who looked to be close. Her parents were obviously religious, so I can understand that if and when Rosalie found herself pregnant, abortion wouldn't have been on the table. But they also seem like the sort of family who would support their daughter and help her raise the baby. Or at least help her find a family to adopt her."

Jemma continued to surf around. "I found a link to some old sermons on the webpage, and it does look as if Pastor Watts tended toward subjects relating to fire and brimstone. If I had to guess, Rosalie's father was conservative in his approach to religion. It's clear that he cared about his parishioners, and both he and his wife lived a life of service, but that doesn't mean he would have taken kindly to his only daughter having a baby out of wedlock."

"So maybe she ran away, or maybe her parents kicked her out. She was seventeen when she came to Gooseberry Bay that summer. She might have turned eighteen, and her parents might have set her loose to sink or swim on her own." I paused and then continued. "There's no way to know why, even if Rosalie Watts actually is Ellery's biological mother, she made the decision to abandon her baby the way she did."

"Unless we find her and ask her," Jemma pointed out.

"Yes," I agreed. "Unless we find Rosalie and ask her."

Jemma continued to look for additional information while I decided to call Ellery. While I was on the phone with my client, Parker called to let Jemma know that she'd picked up Kalen's video game console from Kalen's mother since she never had made it to the Rambling Rose and would bring it by in about an hour. My client was excited about the progress we'd been able to make, but I could tell by the tone of her voice that Ellery was getting nervous now that we had a name. She shared that while she really did want contact information if we could find it, she didn't want us actually contacting Rosalie. She wanted to give the situation some more thought before reaching out. I agreed to this, and I also agreed to let her know if we came up with anything concrete like an address or phone number or even a married last name.

"My client would like us to try to obtain an address or phone number, but she doesn't want us to actually contact the woman at this point," I shared with Jemma.

"I get it. Looking for answers that seem impossible to find is a different decision than actually acting on those answers."

"Do you think we can find anything current for this woman?"

Jemma nodded. "Assuming that she remained in Seattle and didn't move to another town or state, I should be able to track down a marriage certificate, if one exists, through the county records. Just give me a few minutes."

"If we can get a current name, we can do a search for a current address or at least a current email. That sort of thing seems to be widely available on the web."

"Exactly."

Jemma continued to type, and I stood next to her and waited.

"It looks like Rosalie Watts married Jeremiah Langston in August of two thousand and five." She continued to type. "I found a wedding announcement which tells me that Jeremiah was a native of Spokane, Washington and that he worked at a welding shop with his father." She talked and typed at the same time. "I found a phone number for Langston Iron Works. If nothing else, you should be able to track Rosalie down through that. I'm going to look for something more specific to her, however, so give me another minute or two."

Jemma continued to type, and I continued to wait.

"I got it." Jemma sat back. "Rosalie is a real estate agent. She has her cell number and her email listed on her website. I'll forward everything to you, and you can pass it on to your client."

To say that Ellery was thrilled with the information we'd been able to dig up was putting it mildly. She still wasn't sure if she would use the information to reach out, but at least she had a place to start. I asked her to call or email me if she ever contacted Rosalie. I felt pretty confident that we'd tracked down the right person, but until someone actually spoke to Rosalie, we wouldn't know for sure. Ellery agreed to stay in touch, and I wished her well.

By the time Parker arrived, Jemma and I were ready to switch gears and focus on the missing boys. Josie had come home as well, so she grabbed a snack and joined us at the dining table.

Luckily, Jemma was able to easily access Kalen's video game console. It was a newer model, and like Zane's, there was a window for messaging as well as access to various files relating to a variety of different games. The user log showed that End Days was the only game Kalen had been logged into for the past couple of months. It also showed that, like Zane, he's spent a lot of time climbing through the levels.

"So, how can this help us?" Josie asked. "I get that this proves that two of the missing boys seemed to be obsessed with a specific online multiplayer game, and it's reasonable to assume that we'd find a similar pattern on Trevor's video game console if we had access to it. But how does this help us figure out what happened to them or where they might be now?"

Jemma sat back in her chair. She didn't speak, but she did seem to be considering Josie's question.

"Okay, so we know that Zane, Kalen, and Trevor were all into this game big time," Parker said. "It looks like they began working together as allies of some sort after climbing to level fifteen, where presumably the game changes in some way. Do we know how the game changes?"

"Not really," Jemma said. "From what I understand, the quests are single-player challenges until you reach level fifteen, and then players either group themselves or are grouped in some way by the game, and the challenge is to work together. Maybe we need to find someone who has played the game to obtain additional information."

"Were there other players logged in when the three missing boys were logged in?" I asked.

"Sure," Jemma said. "A lot of players seemed to be logged in at any given time." She frowned. "I was going to try to use Zane's account to reach out and contact some of the others, but I never got that far. Maybe we can send a message to one of the other players who've been mentioned and see if they'll respond."

"I remember the names Zork, Halo, Nomad, and Reaper," I said.

"Reaper was the one who was supposed to meet with Zane, Kalen, and Trevor. I have a weird feeling about that," Jemma said. "Let's try the other three."

"What are you going to say?" I asked.

She looked at the screen. "I think I'm going to say that I'm a friend of Zane's who knows he's missing and is trying to track him down. I think I'll just ask if the gamers I contact are willing to talk to me. I'm not sure they'll want to chat in person, but the message board used in the game is too public, so I'll create a private chat room for them to log into. I just have this feeling that there's a predator out there using this game to recruit kids for one reason or another."

"What reason?" Josie asked.

"I don't know," Jemma admitted as she typed.

"Did you share what we've found out with Deputy Todd?" I asked Parker.

"I did. The man seemed unimpressed by my research. According to Todd, there seems to be evidence that the three boys planned to run away together. I guess he found texts to support this. And that may be what happened, but if the boys planned to run away, why didn't they just meet up and go? Why spread things out over three days?"

"Maybe they wanted to make it look more like an abduction than a runaway type situation," Josie suggested.

"Maybe," Parker agreed.

"I feel like both scenarios could be true," Jemma said. "It seems to me that if there is a *someone* who is using the game to recruit kids, then this someone might convince these kids to run away."

"Run away to where?" I asked.

Jemma shrugged. "I don't know. Maybe a commune. Maybe the person who's using the game to recruit teenage boys is a cult leader of some sort."

"Okay," Parker said. "Then how do we put a face to this guru?"

"It seems that the key to finding out who might be using the game would be to find someone else who has made it to the upper levels of the game," I said.

"What about one of the kids who were on the other two teams the guy at the comic book and video game store mentioned," Jemma wondered. "One team is based in New Mexico, and the other is in California."

"Do you have a way to track them down?" I asked.

"Maybe. Give me a minute. I'm going to message Zork, Nomad, and Halo first to see if I can get one of them to respond. Once I do that, I'll see if I can find anything relating to the two teams who reached the final level before the team from Gooseberry Bay."

After several hours of phishing, Jemma was still unable to track down the real names of the three individuals from New Mexico who had completed the game, but she had found their usernames. Two of the three usernames were no longer being used in any game that she could find, but one of the usernames, Xenon 1426, had been used recently in another multiplayer game that Kalen had played from time to time. Taking a chance that the Xenon 1426, who was currently playing Ultimate War, was also the Xenon 1426 who was part of the team to make it to the final level of End Days, Jemma messaged him. No one answered for a good half hour, but eventually, Jemma received a reply.

"So what are you going to say to this person?" Parker asked. "Are you going to pretend to be a player looking for information?"

"No. I think I'm going to pretend to be Ainsley and tell Xenon 1426 that I'm a private investigator trying to find a missing teen. This may scare the kid away, assuming that Xenon 1426 is a kid, which is not something we know with any degree of certainty, but if no one from this group has leaked the details of how the game works beyond a certain level by now, then someone has convinced them to keep what they know to themselves."

Jemma typed out her response to Xenon 1426's inquiry and waited. After a few minutes, a link to a chat room appeared. Jemma followed it. Once she was logged into the chat room, she explained about the game and the missing boys and wondered if the person she was chatting with was one of the first three to conquer the game, End Days. Eventually, Xenon 1426 answered that he was. He asked what she wanted to know. Jemma explained that we really just wanted to track down the three missing boys and that it was our belief that the game might have had something to do with their disappearance. She asked if he was willing to share his experience with the final levels. He messaged back that he was sworn to secrecy as to the content of the final levels, but Xenon 1426 would say that after the final level was reached and conquered, he and the other two players on his team were issued an invitation to meet with someone named Reaper. Apparently, this Reaper was going to give them something of great value as a reward for staying the course and coming so far.

"Did they meet?" Josie asked.

"No," Jemma said. "They planned to meet. They even set up a time and date and everything, but then the boys were involved in an auto accident on the way to the meet. The boy who was driving was injured and was taken to the hospital. The other two were fine, but by the time they were checked out and released, they'd missed the meeting. Reaper never reached out to them again."

"So this Xenon 1426 had no idea what this person going by Reaper was actually after?" I asked.

Jemma shook her head. "He says no. He just said that they were promised some sort of reward, and they were to meet with this Reaper at the designated time and place in order to collect the reward. They were late, Reaper wasn't there, and no one ever reached out again. When they logged into the game after the missed meeting, the game had reset itself, and all three players were back on level one. I guess they talked about starting again, but the friend in the hospital was there for several days, and by the time he got out, they decided to move on to something else."

"I'm totally freaked out that the meeting that was set up as a result of mastering all the levels in the game was an in-person meeting," Parker said.

"Me too," I agreed.

Jemma thanked Xenon 1426 and logged out. He wasn't willing to share any details of the game, so asking those sorts of questions was a dead-end, and it really did seem that he'd told her everything he knew about Reaper.

"We need to take a closer look at all the messages to and from Reaper on both Zane and Kalen's video game consoles," I said. "And we need to try harder to get Trevor's."

"I'll call his mom right now," Josie said. "One way or another, I'll convince her to give it to us."

Chapter 14

The four of us worked late into the night, trying to figure out who Reaper was and whether or not the meeting that was being set up the previous weekend had already occurred. It most likely had. The question was, why exactly had this Reaper wanted to meet face to face with the boys, and what had he done to or with them once they'd met.

Parker had decided to take another stab at Deputy Todd. She explained what we'd found and what we suspected. She shared that Todd seemed reluctant to consider the kidnapping or cult leader theories, but by the time she left his office to join us on the peninsula, he agreed to take another look at things.

"So if the boys all planned to meet this Reaper, why did they go missing at different times?" Josie asked.

"What if the boys made it to the final level on Friday night," Jemma jumped in. "We know they had a marathon session that actually went into Saturday morning, so maybe they were close, and they knew it. They wanted to finish, and then when they did manage to beat the final level, Reaper contacted them and set up the meeting. We know that Reaper had been chatting with the boys for a couple weeks, so at this point, I have to assume he was monitoring their progress and baiting the trap by promising them something when they finished."

"Okay, so what then?" Parker asked.

Our conversation was halted when Jemma heard from Halo, who was unwilling to give his real name but did admit that he was a Gooseberry local who knew the three boys who went missing. He knew a meeting had been set up with Reaper but wasn't sure where the meeting was supposed to take place, but he had talked to Trevor, who'd shared with him that an in-person meeting wasn't really within his comfort zone, so he hadn't intended to show up.

"At this point, I'm going to assume the meeting was set for Saturday. Of course, the only teen to go missing on Saturday was Kalen, but according to Halo, Trevor knew that whatever the prize at the end of the rainbow was, it required an in-person meeting, and he'd already told Halo he wasn't interested in anything like that, so maybe Zane felt the same way. Perhaps Kalen was the only one of the three who was willing to attend an in-person meeting Saturday, so he went alone."

"And then?" Josie asked.

"And then when he got there, he found out that Reaper was only interested in bestowing the reward on the team as a whole, so he enlisted Kalen to convince the other two to show up." I took a stab at an explanation.

"Exactly," Jemma said. "Kalen goes to work on Zane and Trevor. Maybe he finally talks Zane into it, and Zane meets up with Kalen Sunday. It sounds like Reaper still wants Trevor, so the other two ask him to meet them, which could be the meetup the man on the boat saw."

"And then?" Josie asked.

"Maybe Trevor still won't budge and goes home, so someone, probably Kalen, intercepts Trevor on his way home from school Monday and either convinces him to change his mind or maybe they forcibly take him to Reaper."

"Okay. I'm following," Parker said. "But once all three boys are together, then what?"

"I'm not sure," Jemma said. "I suspect that Reaper might have had a boat. We know that Kalen's dirt bike was found in the parking lot near the marina, and Zane headed out on a paddleboard, so maybe he met up with the boat somewhere. I don't know why he would have left his paddleboard in the water, but for now, let's just say he had a reason for doing so. If Reaper was in a boat and his intent was to take the boys somewhere, they could be anywhere by now."

"We talked about a cult," I reminded the group. "There are a lot of private islands in the area. If I was a cult leader, I would think that a private island was a good place to set up camp."

"Of course, the first group of boys lived in New Mexico. If they had made the meeting with Reaper, he wouldn't have been on a boat," Parker pointed out. She looked at Jemma. "When you chatted with Halo, was he willing to tell you anything about the game?"

She nodded. "Halo's team hasn't reached as high a level as the missing kids had, but basically, he told me that while the first fourteen levels are mostly a singular quest, once you reach level fifteen, you are assigned to a team. The point of the game from that point on is to work as a team. All three players need to be logged on for anyone to play, so he assumes the game has a way of knowing which players live near the others."

"Okay," I said. "So you're put on a team, then what?"

"Then the team is dropped into a post-apocalyptic world with challenges to meet. There are mutants who want to kill you, acid rain, giant bugs, and man-eating reptiles. You are dropped into this world without food, water, or shelter, all of which you need to find quickly. If you don't find water before the clock ticks down, you are dead. If you don't find food or eat the wrong thing, you are dead. If you don't have shelter and a giant bug or man-eating reptile eats you, you are dead. If one person on the team dies, the game restarts for the entire team, so you have to be as invested in watching everyone else's back as you are in watching your own."

"So the game teaches team building and cooperation," I said.

"Yes, it seems to," Jemma agreed. "It also teaches survival skills. If the team comes across a berry bush, they must decide if it's edible or if it's toxic. They don't have Google in this world, so they have to find other ways of getting their answers. In a way, it sounds like a game that might teach some valuable skills."

"I take it the higher you climb, the more difficult the obstacles," Josie stated.

"That would seem to be the case. Halo said that if at any point it appears as if the team isn't working together, there are penalties. This isn't the sort of game you can win or even play on your own."

"So what now?" Josie asked. "We have to assume the meet-up took place, so whatever was going to happen to the group has happened to them. How do we figure out what that was?"

"There is the team from California who also won the game," I reminded the gang. "Maybe we can find out what happened to them."

"I haven't been able to find real or usernames for this group yet, but I'll keep trying," Jemma said.

I think at this point, we all felt sort of stuck, but we had made progress. Still, assuming we were on the right track with the game and the face-to-face meeting that could very well have led to a kidnapping, where were we to go from here? If this Reaper had kidnapped the boys, then chances are they were long gone by now.

It wasn't until later that afternoon that Jemma was finally able to track down one of the three team members from the group in California.

"So, did this guy know anything?" I asked the minute Jemma ended the chat session.

"He did. He told me that like the group in New Mexico and the group in Gooseberry Bay, once his team beat the final level and had the final key, they were offered a face-to-face meeting with someone named Reaper. They were told they would receive a valuable prize for completing the game but that they had to show up in person. The kid I spoke to, who finally shared that he was a sixteen-year-old named Carl, told me that the two other guys on his team didn't want to meet with this random guy no matter how cool the prize might be, so he went alone. When he arrived, he was told that the prize was only available to the team as a whole. The man who showed up told Carl that if he could get the other two members of the team on board, he'd give them a chance and set up a second meeting. Carl shared that he really wanted to find out what the prize was since he just knew it would be something awesome, so he agreed to talk to his friends, and a second meeting was set up for all three to meet with Reaper. Once Carl met with the others, they managed to convince him that the whole thing seemed creepy, so none of them showed up for the second meeting. Like the first group, all their games reset to the first level at this point."

"So if this Carl met with Reaper, then he can describe him," Josie pointed out.

"Sort of. Reaper wore a black mask that covered the lower portion of his face. Carl described the guy as tall, at least six foot five, with black eyes and black hair. He said he was thin, and his complexion appeared to be pale, although he could only see a strip of flesh between the mask and his hairline. He wore black clothing, black shoes, and a black cape. Carl said that Reaper reminded him of Zorro."

"Doesn't sound like a lot to go on," I admitted.

"It doesn't, but the man did have a distinctive ring. The ornament was worn on the man's right hand and featured four small circles overlapping in the center. The way Carl described it, I pictured a Venn diagram. One circle, the one at the top, was gold and held no stone. The other three circles were silver. One of the silver circles had a small black stone, while one had a green stone, and the other stone was red."

"So, if we can find the ring, maybe we can find the man," I said.

"Sounds like a longshot," Parker commented.

"It sounds pretty near impossible," Jemma admitted, "but unless anyone has a better idea…"

We all agreed we didn't, so Jemma got to work searching the World Wide Web for some trace of the man we believed had taken three innocent kids for reasons we could only guess at.

Chapter 15

Either by luck or by fate, Jemma was actually able to track down someone who recognized the ring once she'd posted a sketch in every relevant chat room she could think of. The man who hit her back told her that a man named Darryl Quinn, who lived on a private island off the coast of Oregon and spent most of his time gaming and attending gaming conventions, owned a ring that fit her description to a T. Apparently, he was also a guru of sorts who'd linked himself to the game through the software the man at the comic book and video game store showed us after he'd discovered that the game taught many of the same lessons in self-reliance and teamwork he tried to teach his followers.

Even though we'd figured out who the man was and where he could probably be found, we weren't equipped to storm the island and rescue the kids, so Parker took all the evidence we'd managed to gather, along with the theory we'd worked up and once again went to talk to Deputy Todd. This time, he took things seriously and called in the FBI, which I thought he'd done in the beginning, but hadn't. The FBI located the island, and by the end of the day, all three boys had been found.

The thing I found the most surprising was that all three boys had ended up voluntarily going with Darryl. Once he had them on board his boat, he made them see that the only way out of the pain they'd found themselves living in was to take back their power and learn to make their own decisions. Reaper used the lessons learned through the game to convince them that they had what it took to take care of themselves, even in a hostile environment.

Of course, even though the man had been able to talk the kids into voluntarily going with him, they were only fifteen, so he was arrested for kidnapping and would face trial at some point in the future. I still wasn't sure why he'd targeted the boys or how he knew what was going on in each player's life. I wasn't sure why he insisted on having all three boys on board before making his offer of asylum either, but it did seem that teamwork was a big theme with him.

All of the other followers living on the island were adults who chose to be there, so they hadn't proved to be a threat to Darryl's freedom. The fact that he seemed to have targeted minors seemed odd to us, but I supposed he must have had his reasons. The boys all reported that they'd been treated well during their stay, but I supposed that might have changed if they'd been there longer.

Josie had to work today, and Parker had a story to file, so it was just Jemma and me who met to talk things over.

"The fact that this man sought out three fifteen-year-olds and then convinced them to go with him is super creepy, but after we identified the man, I took a look at exactly what he is doing on that island," she said.

"And?"

"And in theory, the ideas he teaches are pretty functional. He's big into the concept of being part of a team and the game, which he apparently helped develop, only allows for a team to succeed. If one member of the team goes off on their own, the entire team suffers, but if the team works together to make decisions and handle any work that needs to be accomplished, they flourish. Of course, the idea of teamwork and selflessness when interacting with a team isn't a new concept. It's been around for years, but there aren't a lot of people who are really adept at putting others before themselves and working for the greater good rather than focusing on what is best for each individual."

"I wonder what will happen to the colony on the island now that Daryl is in jail."

Jemma shrugged. "I suppose if Daryl did a good job teaching teamwork and group survival, the men and women who live there will be able to figure it out. It is an interesting social experiment. Actually, I kind of like the part of the game that dictates that if one team member dies in the game, all the team members die. It seems like a good lesson in watching the back of your fellow man as well as your own."

"Yeah. The man seemed to have insight, but he was crazy. Any stable adult would know you can't just recruit a group of kids to join your little cult and not find yourself in a whole lot of hot water." I paused and looked out the window at the bay. "Have you heard if the boys came home willingly, or were they upset to leave?"

"I'm not sure. I guess if the boys didn't want to leave, their parents are going to need to keep an eye on them. It seems to me they might prove to be a high risk for running away again. I get that they were coerced to run the first time, but now that they've had a taste of freedom..."

"Yeah. I can see someone like Zane chucking it all and trying again on his own. Kalen too, for that matter."

Jemma got up and grabbed a couple bottles of water. She handed me one. "So now that you've solved Cora's case by helping to find Zane and you've solved Ellery's case by identifying the woman who most likely owned the charm bracelet, what's next for you?"

"I actually got a call this morning from a man who wants to track down his daughter. She's an adult, not a kid, so I'll need to consider things carefully. I'd hate to put a father and daughter in touch with each other if the daughter doesn't want to be found."

"So, what's this guy's story?"

"He said that he and his daughter fought when she was just eighteen, and she took off. He never saw or heard from her again, but he's tracked her to Gooseberry Bay. He doesn't necessarily think she's here now, but she was here a year ago, and he's hoping I can pick up her trail. Like I said, I'm hesitant. This young woman might have a good reason to want to avoid the man. Still, he told me that his wife has been diagnosed with cancer, and while she's getting treatment and her prognosis is good, having to face a life-and-death situation has made him realize that it's time for the silly fight with his daughter to end."

"I guess you can track the girl down and explain things. If she wants to reconnect with her parents, it can be her call."

I took a sip of my water. "That's what I was thinking. I'm going to meet with the man in person Thursday. I guess I'll decide what to do then."

Jemma and I decided to take a walk. It was a gorgeous day, and it seemed that the dogs were feeling antsy. It was nice to have friends to share the everyday moments of my life with. I didn't come to Gooseberry Bay looking for friends, but at this point, I didn't know what I'd do without them.

Chapter 16

It had been two weeks since we'd found Rosalie, and it almost two weeks since we'd figured out how a seemingly innocent video game had led to recruitment for a real-world cult. Adam had called to let me know he was back in town, and we had plans to meet for lunch so I could fill him in on everything he'd missed while he'd been away.

In the meantime, I'd decided to go for a long walk along the waterline with the dogs. Like most days in Gooseberry Bay, the weather was absolutely perfect. I'd let the dogs take a long swim, and we were on our way back to the cottage when Ellery called.

"Ellery. It's so good to hear your voice. How are things?" I asked.

"Really good. I finally decided to be brave and call Rosalie."

"And?" I asked.

"I briefly explained the reason for my call, and after a much longer stretch of silence than I was comfortable with, she eventually began to cry. Once we got past that, I explained in detail who I was and why I'd tracked her down. I shared that I had the charm bracelet, and I shared the details of my trip to Gooseberry Bay, looking for answers. When I finally got around to the details of how we'd ended up with her name, she admitted that she had been the one who abandoned a baby in a church north of Seattle."

"So, are you going to meet?" I asked, hoping that the woman didn't simply tell her that she was uninterested in a relationship and blow her off.

"We are; next weekend. Rose said that her family doesn't know about me, so she's coming to me so we can really talk. She admitted that it is a complicated situation and that she needs to figure out how to handle things, but she very much wants to meet me."

"That's wonderful, Ellery. I'm glad it all worked out."

"We still have some things to figure out, but I feel like a huge gap in my life has been closed. I really can't thank you enough."

"No need to thank me. I was happy to help. Did Rosalie tell you why she left you in a church?"

"She told me that her parents were super strict and that her dad tended to rule with an iron fist. He was a preacher by trade, but he was the sort of preacher who was all about penance and punishment. Rose told me that it was her opinion that her father simply ignored all the parts of the Bible that weren't directly related to those topics. In his world, there was no room for tolerance or forgiveness."

"That sounds awful," I said.

"That's what I thought," Ellery shared. "Rose told me that she was just seventeen when she got pregnant. She also shared that by the time she found out she was pregnant, the father of the baby, who'd been in the Navy, had shipped out. Rose was all alone and couldn't go to her family, so she ran away. She wanted the baby to be raised in a kind and loving Christian family, and she wanted to be sure her parents would never know about the baby, so she decided to leave me in a church that she'd attended a few times in the past. Rose told me she loved me and hated to leave me, but she also assured me that if her father had found out about me, he would have forced her to let him raise me in his house of hatred and intolerance, and that was something she'd never allow. She admitted that there might have been a better way to go about things, but she did what she knew to do at the time and then prayed that her baby would find the sort of family she'd always wished she'd had. She was happy to hear that I adored my adoptive parents and couldn't have asked for a better childhood."

Ellery and I chatted for over an hour before she said that she had to go. I was happy with the way things had worked out, and she'd told me that she was happy as well. I knew that Adam would be by to pick me up for our lunch date in just over an hour, so once I'd arrived at the cottage, I headed inside to get ready.

"I've missed you," I said, hugging the handsome man who stood on my doorstep.

"I've missed you as well." He took a step back and then asked, "Are you ready?"

"I am. Just let me grab my purse."

During our meal, Adam asked lots of questions, and I caught him up on both the case of the missing boys and the case of the found charm bracelet. He seemed interested and offered input when appropriate, but I could tell he had something on his mind. Once I'd caught him up, I asked about his trip. He provided the details, but it felt like he was simply reciting the contents of his calendar. Adam and I knew each other well enough that most of the awkwardness we'd experienced at first seemed to be gone, so why the awkward lunch?

"Is everything okay?" I asked.

"Everything is fine. I guess I'm just a bit jet-lagged."

"I guess that's understandable. You did have a whirlwind trip. Did you make it to England to visit your family?"

"No, not on this trip. I did, however, speak to Amber and Kent Wentworth while I was on the east coast."

"Really? Amber and Kent are Marilee's parents."

He nodded.

"Did they have any insight as to what might have happened to her?"

"They told me that Marilee was somehow involved with a man named Dillinger Fagan, and the last time they spoke to Marilee, she was on her way to Rio with the guy."

"Rio? I thought she was supposed to be taking care of Avery and me."

"Kent and Amber thought that as well. Everyone in the family did, but Marilee told everyone, including them, that she didn't think the children were safe with her, so she'd found friends who were willing to take temporary custody. When Amber initially tried to talk Marilee into bringing Ava and Avery to Massachusetts so she and Kent could look out for them, Marilee refused. Once Marilee left for Rio, her parents never heard from her again. Amber told me that she tried to figure out what Marilee had done with the two little girls, but there was no trace of either child once the group left Piney Point. She tried to track down Wilma as well, but her attempts were unsuccessful."

"Did Amber know about the money? Did she know that Warren was putting twenty grand into accounts for Avery and me?"

"No, Amber said that Marilee never mentioned any money. Keep in mind that Marilee had everyone convinced that Warren was the bad guy."

"It sounds like it was actually Marilee who was the bad guy in this story."

"Yeah," Adam agreed. "Kent and Amber have admitted that things were handled poorly from the beginning. They admitted that they should have personally made sure that you and Avery were cared for rather than depending on Marilee to handle things. They admitted that after Marilee left you at Piney Point, they should have flown out and taken over custody. I could tell that they felt awful about the way things turned out. When I told them about the money and that Marilee had apparently lied about Warren in order to take the money and run, they felt really awful."

Part of me wondered why they hadn't done more, but another part of me knew that dwelling on the past wouldn't do me a bit of good. "Did they know why Marilee left me with the cop who raised me, which seems to be what happened since he had the photo of Marilee with Avery and me, and he apparently knew my real birthday? He may even have had my real birth certificate."

"They didn't know for sure, but they did say that Marilee lived in Savannah for two years when she was fresh out of high school. Amber assumes she must have met your dad then. I told Amber that the man you ended up with was a cop, and she shared that Marilee had a roommate whose brother was a cop but didn't know his name."

"My dad didn't have a sister."

"Maybe your dad was friends with the brother, and they met somehow. Maybe when Marilee was looking for someone to hand you off to, she came up with a story about you being in danger and handed you off to the cop who raised you. That story does make more sense than him finding you in a burning building."

I frowned. "That does make more sense. What doesn't make sense is that my dad came up with the burning building thing in the first place. There has to be a reason for the elaborate lie."

"I agree with that. But given the fact that your father is dead and Marilee is long gone, I'm not sure how we're ever going to unwind that part of the story."

I took a sip of my iced tea and then leaned back in my chair. "If Marilee did, in fact, know my dad, and if she did indeed hand me off to him, then who did she hand Avery off to? If we can get a list of everyone Marilee knew, perhaps we can figure that part of the story out. That's the part of the whole thing that means the most to me. If I can find Avery, I'm not sure I'll even care if I don't unwind the rest."

"I can ask Amber to come up with a list. I'm sure she'll have names we can start with. People Marilee knew in school. People she worked with. While it is a longshot, I agree that digging into Marilee's past seems like as good an idea as any at this point."

Adam agreed to call Amber once he got home and could look up the number. Once we'd finished our meal, we headed back to the cottage. I'd planned to spend the whole day with Adam, but he really did seem tired. While I knew that he genuinely wanted to help me, I think in some way, my search for answers had put him in an awkward position with his family. It seemed that they'd all dropped the ball. I imagined that having someone constantly bring that fact up couldn't be pleasant.

I offered Adam a drink when we got back to the cottage, but he declined. He promised to call me tomorrow, but he did confess that he needed to get some sleep before he fell asleep on his feet. I kissed him on the cheek and wished him sweet dreams, and then I went inside. I couldn't help but wonder if Marilee was still alive. If she had taken off and was still present in the world, then maybe I could find her. Finding her really was my best chance at finding Avery. I wasn't sure how I'd go about tracking this woman down, but I knew her name, and I knew who she was with when she headed for Rio a quarter of a century ago. That wasn't a lot, but it was a place to start, and lately, I'd found that as long as you had a place to start and you had brilliant friends willing to help you, the rest eventually fell into place.

USA Today best-selling author Kathi Daley lives in beautiful Lake Tahoe with her husband, Ken. When she isn't writing, she likes spending time hiking the miles of desolate trails surrounding her home. She's authored more than a hundred and fifty books in thirteen series. Find out more about her books at www.kathidaley.com

Made in the USA
Middletown, DE
23 March 2021

36123990R00113